SEEKER

DOVE SEASON

ROBIN BRANDE

RYER PUBLISHING

SEEKER
(Dove Season)
By Robin Brande

Published by Ryer Publishing
www.ryerpublishing.com
Copyright 2025 by Robin Brande
www.robinbrande.com
Cover art by cappa/Deposit Photos
Cover design by Ryer Publishing
All rights reserved.
Print ISBN: 978-1-952383-27-4
Ebook ISBN: 978-1-952383-06-9

ALSO BY ROBIN BRANDE

<u>Dove Season Universe</u>

Dove Season

Finder

Seeker

Believer

Maker

Explorer

<u>Winnie Parsons Mysteries</u>

The Genius Track

A Man of Appetites

A Drop of Sweat

The Long Gray Hook

The Slip of a Rib

<u>Parallelogram Quartet</u>

Into the Parallel

Caught in the Parallel

Seize the Parallel

Beyond the Parallel

Young Adult

Evolution, Me & Other Freaks of Nature

Fat Cat

Doggirl

Replay

Bradamante Saga

Book of Earth

Book of Water

Romance

Love Proof

Freefall

Heart of Ice

Fire and Ice

Collections

The Love of a Good Dog

Mountain Tough

The Miraculous Unknown

Self-Help

What If You're Doing It Right?

What If You're Doing It Right? For Teens

CONTENTS

DOVE SEASON UNIVERSE
RECOMMENDED READING ORDER

Dove Season

Finder

Seeker

Believer

Maker

Explorer

SEEKER

TUCSON 1971

1

The meeting was about to come to order. Travis Baird sat on a folding metal chair in back, even though he knew he would be called to the front eventually. A buzz had gone through the group of fourteen when he walked in. Enough of them knew who he was, and those who did quickly spread the word to those who didn't.

Travis wondered what they saw when they looked at him. A skinny, frail-looking scientist, maybe close to fifty. The thinning gray hair gave his age away.

But Travis Baird was only thirty-two. Wasting away. Dying.

A side effect of his job. Of the things he kept finding. Artifacts and organisms left behind by what he knew were alien aircraft, no matter how the government and Air Force tried to explain them away.

The meeting was in the back of a storefront, a Mexican gift shop during the day. But the inventory of colorful pottery and turquoise jewelry and bright ladies' tops and dresses probably never got refreshed. Someone might buy something, and the owner of the shop, Mercedes Fuentes, probably shifted around the remaining merchandise so it wouldn't look like there was an empty space.

Because the storeroom where Travis now sat held very few items. No replacement clothing or pottery or hand-loomed rugs. There were a couple of stacks of wire shelves, but they held mostly Styrofoam coffee cups and small paper plates. Enough to supply the ACRO group, the Alien Contact Research Organization, through a year's worth of monthly meetings. Two years if there were only fourteen regular attendees like tonight.

Travis looked around, but he couldn't find any evidence of the other work Mercedes Fuentes did. Maybe she kept her typewriter and the reams of paper she went through at home, in a den. Maybe she only typed at night. It made sense, because otherwise customers might hear and wonder. What was this nice Mexican lady with the cute little gift shop doing back there tap, tap, tapping away? Hello, excuse me, do you have this blouse in another size?

The back storage space wasn't very roomy, but Mercedes had managed to cram in here twenty brass-colored folding metal chairs in four rows of five.

There was a square card table at the rear of the room that Mercedes had covered with a bright red tablecloth. A large silver coffee urn sat on top. Styrofoam cups sat in a stack in front of it along with a plate of sugar cubes and a small Mexican pottery pitcher filled with milk or cream.

There was food, too. A pecan coffee cake on a large paper

plate, already shaved down to a quarter of its original size by the hungry guests. Another paper plate held portions of a long salami submarine sandwich that had been cut into one-inch chunks. It was more than Travis got at other meetings, especially anything run by the government. They didn't like to feed their outside contractors. Particularly when those contractors weren't telling them what they wanted to hear.

There were only two sandwich portions left. Travis took one along with a slice of coffee cake and loaded them onto a paper cocktail plate. He filled a Styro cup with the dark, rich-smelling coffee out of the silver urn, then found a seat in back and settled down to wait.

As sick as he was, he still had some appetite. And he hadn't eaten since a few pieces of toast and coffee at a diner this morning. This was an unsanctioned trip, so he was paying for it himself. That meant being careful about his expenses.

He was grateful for the free food, but now that he had it in front of him, he didn't think he could eat it after all. His stomach had felt clenched all day, anticipating tonight's meeting.

Travis wasn't sure how to handle himself. What to say. How best to approach Mercedes Fuentes with what he had learned about her just a few days ago. He hoped some idea would come to him during the meeting.

She was an attractive, well-groomed woman with an open, friendly face. In her fifties, Travis guessed. She wore her thick brown hair in a bun on top of her head. A few wavy tendrils hung loosely down at the sides, making her look relaxed and approachable.

Above her dark brown skirt and leather sandals, Mercedes wore a bright pink short-sleeved blouse like the ones Travis had seen out front in her shop. It had a flower design embroidered at the top. She wore a silver necklace with a turquoise pendant hanging in the center, and had on a pair of turquoise earrings. All of them were just like the jewelry Travis had seen on display. Mercedes Fuentes was her own best model.

She was the only Mexican member of the group here tonight. (Or maybe Chicano. Travis had heard the term used and wondered if Mercedes might prefer that.) Everyone else at the meeting was as white as Travis.

Some might be surprised to see an important international society like the Alien Contact Research Organization run by a woman, and a Mexican woman at that. But Travis wasn't surprised. Mercedes Fuentes probably knew more than any of the high-level scientists who belonged to ACRO. She might not have their PhDs, but she had something much more.

In addition to running the organization with an efficiency people admired, Mercedes was also the editor and chief author of the Alien Contact Research Organization Bulletin, published every month. Travis subscribed and read it cover to cover as soon as it came.

In every issue Mercedes Fuentes provided details of the latest alien sightings reported around the world. Her sources included ACRO member-scientists on every continent except Antarctica. This past month there were reports from Venezuela, Brazil, Denmark, France ... and also a small town called Red Rock, Arizona, about thirty miles north-west of Tucson.

That was why Travis had come here. Hopeful.

He wondered why the other people at this meeting were here. Who were they? Curiosity-seekers? Scientists? Possibly even someone who had been abducted? Travis knew abductees were around, congregating, talking. He couldn't tell if anyone in the group was one of them just by looking.

The youngest was a girl in her twenties in cut-offs and a ratty T-shirt. The oldest was a woman probably in her eighties dressed conservatively like a grandmother. In between were men and women of varying ages, some of them dressed casually, some in what looked like work clothes. Travis wasn't the only man wearing a tie.

He wanted to look official, like someone had sent him here. He dressed like he usually did whenever he worked in his lab at Colorado State University in Fort Collins. Tan slacks, light blue button-down shirt, red and blue striped tie, loafers. He left his navy blue jacket back in the motel room. Too hot. Even at the beginning of September, the daytime temps in Tucson were still around a hundred.

Back home in Fort Collins, Travis's wife Rosie and their daughter Caroline would already be enjoying the cooler autumn weather and the yellowing aspen leaves. Travis missed them. Terribly. He had been away from them too long. Eleven days so far, spent chasing down one lead after another. So far without success.

But maybe tonight would be different. Maybe Mercedes Fuentes was the key.

Travis wondered if the other people here tonight knew

what she could do. He suspected not. If Mercedes had let it be widely known that she could communicate telepathically with alien races, there would be far too many attendees at her meetings than could fit in a small back storeroom.

Travis only knew because a few days ago he had received a tip from one of his sources in New Mexico. She called his house and left a message with Rosie. Travis called her back from his motel room in Tucson the next day, and she said she knew where he was, and why. She had seen it in a vision. She told him that Mercedes Fuentes had certain abilities, much like hers, and that Travis should go to tonight's meeting and ask her for help. His source had already sent Mercedes a telepathic message that Travis was a good man, and he was safe to talk to.

Travis had no idea if the communication worked or whether it might be enough. But he knew he had to try.

He had to approach Mercedes cautiously. She might not like that he knew. She might not be willing to help him. But Travis hoped to heaven she would.

His daughter Caroline's seventh birthday was just a few days away. Travis absolutely had to be back for it. But he hoped from the bottom of his soul that he wouldn't have to go home empty-handed. That this trip wouldn't turn out to be a waste of time.

Travis didn't have much time anymore. He couldn't afford to waste a single day.

A few minutes after seven o'clock, four more people entered the store. Mercedes had already put up her *Closed/Cerrado* sign on the door, but they walked on through, straight to the back storeroom without any hesitation.

One of them was a heavy-set man with fine white hair and a thick white mustache. Travis knew him. Robert Cloister. The rancher wore wide jeans, dusty at the cuffs, and a sturdy white cotton button-down shirt tucked in at the waist. He had a substantial leather belt with a big silver buckle in the center and wore dusty, beaten-in cowboy boots.

Robert Cloister scanned the crowd, nodded at few familiar faces, then locked onto Travis sitting in back. Cloister didn't seem that surprised to see him. Travis gave him a nod of acknowledgment. The two of them knew each other, but not well.

Cloister had been the sole witness of a landing out near Picacho Peak, midway between Tucson and Casa Grande. It must have made enough of an impact that two years later he was still coming to meetings like this. It confirmed what Travis thought at the time. That the rancher was a practical, down-to-earth man who had been scared out of his wits by what he saw.

A disk-shaped alien craft had touched down in a fallow field near Cloister's place. Cloister had his binoculars out, watching. The lights in the sky had already attracted his attention about five minutes before. That, and his two hounds baying.

Three figures disembarked from the ship. Cloister could make out what they looked like against the lighted craft.

Travis listened to his report and pretended to ignore the

big rancher shaking. Travis understood how terrifying it was to see a nightmare come to life.

Cloister described them: big, stretched out, maybe taller than six feet.

Weird scaly skin, like alligators.

Or lizards, Travis thought, but he didn't suggest it. Unlike some of his colleagues, he preferred using the official name for the species, RL-40s. But others had come up with more descriptive names, and those were the ones that stuck: Lizard People, or Reptilites. Like all of this was a science fiction movie instead of cold, hard reality.

Cloister also mentioned a feature of the aliens' anatomy that Travis had heard before: they had large hands, about twice the size of a man's, and only three fingers on each one.

"Where did they go?" Travis asked him. "From the ship?"

Cloister had passed a shaking hand over his sweating face. "Damnedest thing. They … they sort of floated off. No, *flew* off. Three different directions. *Fast*. Like shot from guns. Blinked, and they were gone."

"And you didn't see them come back?" Travis had asked him, even though he already guessed the answer. This wasn't his first time of hearing about the RL-40s.

"Nothing to come back to," said Cloister. "Ship took off. Straight up. Blink, and that was gone, too. After that, I …" Cloister shook his head, embarrassed. "I'll admit I didn't stick around."

"No reason to," Travis assured him. "You were right. They don't come back."

The big, tough rancher looked visibly relieved. Travis had gotten to him within forty-eight hours of the event.

Cloister had probably spent the rest of the first night and all of the second staring out his windows into the dark, alert to any sign of the aliens' return.

But what Travis didn't say was that the alternative was worse. The RL-40s were gone, yes—but *where?* Their ships landed on empty fields, and remote country roads, and sometimes pastures where panicking livestock stampeded to get away. Then the aliens disembarked and separated and disappeared into different directions.

And they were still out there, as far as Travis knew. In the last few years of hearing about them, so far no one had reported finding a dead Lizard Man anywhere.

Travis wasn't sorry he hadn't seen a live RL-40 himself. He used to wish for that, for some personal experience after hearing about so much of it second hand. But he finally did have his own encounter with a different species of alien, out near a pond in Las Cruces, New Mexico.

Once had been terrifying enough. That experience had cured him of wanting it ever again.

Until he read about the incident in Red Rock in last month's ACRO Bulletin.

He drove down to Arizona as soon as he could.

"I think that's all of us for tonight," Mercedes Fuentes said to the group. She had an accent that made every English word she spoke sound musical.

While Cloister and the other three newcomers foraged the scraps on the snack table, Mercedes Fuentes strode back into her shop and flipped the lock on her door.

Cloister sat on the empty folding chair next to Travis. The chair sagged beneath his bulk. Travis had lost at least twenty pounds in the last two years, but Cloister must have gained double that. Last time Travis saw him, the rancher looked strong and tough and vital. But time, and probably stress, took their toll on everyone.

Cloister leaned over and muttered, "You boys are fast. Good."

Travis wasn't sure what he meant.

But then Mercedes Fuentes began her meeting, and Travis understood.

"Last night we had another visit from our friends in the Pleiades," she said, naming a cluster of stars visible from Earth. A murmur rolled through the group.

Travis couldn't tell whether Mercedes was excited or upset. She said, "They took somebody else."

2

Colorado was an hour ahead of Arizona this time of year. Eight-thirty AM in Fort Collins was seven-thirty in Tucson, so at least Travis could save that one hour of waiting.

But he had been up since five, too agitated to sleep any more. He parted the drapes in his motel room and verified it was still dark outside.

The diner next door wouldn't open for another hour. Travis filled the time by sitting up in bed and checking over the notes he made last night. He added a few more things he remembered. He wanted to make his written report as complete as possible.

His boss, Dr. Alvin Linsk, head of the Colorado State University biology department, discouraged any of his investigators calling him at home. Travis assumed it was because Linsk didn't want his wife to overhear the kinds of conversations they might have. None of the wives were supposed to know what was going on.

But Travis had told Rosie some of it anyway, just in case. If he wasn't going to be here to take care of her and Caroline, he wanted to make sure Rosie had some warning of what might happen.

At five-fifty he dressed and walked next door to the diner. He was the only customer waiting when the waitress unlocked the door.

"Coffee and toast?" she guessed, brightening the morning with a smile.

She reminded Travis of Rosie. Not as pretty—not by a long shot—but with that same kind of sunny disposition. Rosie had been a waitress when Travis first met her. Even though he could barely afford the habit, he started buying coffee and toast every morning on his way into work at the Colorado State University campus just so he could bask in her beautiful smile. She made every one of Travis's days better. And still did, more than eight years running.

Travis sat at one of the clean Formica-topped tables and stared out the diner window at the oncoming dawn. He rehearsed what he was going to say to Dr. Linsk. He knew Dr. Linsk might be constrained in how much he could say back.

It was a confusing time in Linsk's department right now. For years his various teams had received ample funding from various government and military agencies. But something had shifted inside the Pentagon, and now the Air Force was actively trying to discredit the investigations they had previously paid for.

At the same time, the Department of Defense was still pumping a hundred thousand dollars a year into the biology department's budget, having them come up with plans for how to survive if the United States one day colonized the moon or even Mars.

Travis had once planned on doing only that: studying Mars biology. Figuring out which plants the first wave of settlers could grow in the harsh Martian environment so they could sustain an independent existence.

But his path had veered off in another way.

Sometimes Travis envied the research scientists who went into the campus labs every day, spending their time theorizing and experimenting. Not chasing down alien specimens or seeing people killed from alien contact.

But it was too late to go back. Too late to unknow what he knew. Travis was too addicted now to finding the truth.

He had a second cup of coffee and watched the other customers stream in and out of the diner. Then at seven o'clock he returned to the motel and prepared to make his call.

Dr. Linsk was a punctual man. At seven-thirty Arizona time he answered his phone on the first ring.

"Where are you?" Linsk asked. Travis could hear the tension in his voice. It had been days since he last checked in.

Linsk could have asked Rosie. Travis called her every night. But it went against Linsk's protocol.

"Still in Tucson," Travis said. "Finally got something last night." He took a breath and prepared to lie.

These were confusing times. Travis had to be careful what he said.

As if to remind him, Linsk suddenly changed his tone. "You get your ass back here," he growled at Travis, "or you're fired."

Travis said, "I assume she's listening."

"Damn right," Linsk said.

The secretary who had worked for Dr. Linsk for nearly ten years had surprised her boss a few months ago by handing in her resignation.

She wouldn't meet Linsk's gaze when he asked her why. And then four other secretaries in the department quit, too.

Before Linsk could interview any replacements, the university administration filled all five of the positions.

Within a week Linsk suspected the new secretaries were reporting to someone else. So far Linsk didn't know which particular group was spying on him and his department.

"I'll talk fast," Travis said.

Linsk answered, "I'm sick of your excuses."

"First of all, I need money," Travis said. "It's going to take me another few days."

"Yeah, and what did they say?" Linsk asked.

Travis had the motel room phone book open to the page for Western Union. He read out the address of the closest one.

"Okay, then what did you do?" Linsk asked.

Travis was used to these disjointed conversations. He assumed Dr. Linsk just wrote down the address on a slip of paper. Linsk wouldn't ask his secretary to wire the money, he would do it himself. The whole business of operating the department had gotten much more complicated.

"There's a farm hand out in a town called Red Rock," Travis said. "He claims he was abducted and stayed awake the whole time."

"All right, go on," Linsk said, sounding slightly bored. But Travis knew he was anything but.

"The guy is Mexican," Travis said, "and didn't like me skulking around on my own. But last night I found a translator who can help me. We're going out there tonight to meet with the guy when he gets off work. This one's for real, Al. Maybe the best lead we've ever had."

What Travis didn't say:

The guy was dying, Al. Some kind of cancer. Mercedes Fuentes doesn't know what kind. I read her report in the ACRO Bulletin. She said the guy's doctors said he had just a few months to live.

He was still working, even though some days he was in so much pain he could barely walk. But he needed to feed his family. Then one night last month he was driving home after dark, and he saw lights out over one of the fields not too far in the distance.

Same thing: the weird lights, the strange dome shape, something happening where nothing should.

Our guy parks his truck and stumbles over the dirt and sees a spaceship hovering over the ground.

There are two women standing beneath it. Beautiful women, he told Mercedes. He couldn't walk any further, the pain was so bad.

He fell on the field. He thought he probably passed out. Because the next thing he knew, one of the beautiful women was carrying him in her arms.

She acted like he weighed no more than air. He looked up at her face. It glowed. She looked human, except her eyes were a funny shape. Bigger and wider than they should be, like sideways ovals. They were glowing, too. An eerie silvery blue.

And her hands. There was webbing between her fingers. Like a mermaid, he told Mercedes, like a mermaid from a fairy tale.

Mercedes Fuentes didn't put all of it in the ACRO Bulletin. She told me the rest of it last night. But in the Bulletin she wrote that the aliens used some kind of green light on the man. I knew what that meant the minute I saw it. I'm sure you know too, Al.

These were the Healers. Must be. The green light matches what we've heard from other people. And I saw the guy with my own eyes a few days ago. He was tossing around bales of hay like he had never been sick a day in his life. Mercedes told me the man woke up the next morning after his abduction and was perfectly well.

But everyone who has come across the Healers seems to forget what they looked like after the event. This is the first time we've gotten a full description.

Beautiful women? Webbed hands? Good God. A whole new species. Not like any of the others we've classified.

And if Mercedes Fuentes is right, they come from the Pleiades. She's been communicating with them for years. She says she'll try to find them for me. Maybe even tonight.

And if I meet one, if I meet a Healer, I'm going to ask her shine her green light on me.

I want to live, Al. For me and for Rosie and Caroline.

Travis also didn't tell Linsk about what Mercedes Fuentes said at last night's meeting. About "our friends in the Pleiades" abducting somebody else.

Or that the second abduction was in Red Rock, too.

Travis kept all of that to himself.

He trusted Dr. Alvin Linsk … to a certain degree. Even before Travis started working for him, Linsk had been his mentor.

But there was a lot of money flowing from the government and military these days, and Travis was tired of being surprised by which of his trusted colleagues turned out to be compromised.

He had already caught one of the men he supervised doctoring one of Travis's reports to change some of the facts. When Travis confronted him, the man resigned.

And Ricky Aspell, one of the newest hires on the team, seemed determined to contaminate samples he gathered out in the field. Once might be an accident. But so far, despite Travis going over the procedures again, Ricky had done it at least five more times.

And someone inside the biology department was feeding information to the Air Force's new task force that was trying to debunk what the investigators found.

Until Travis could look Dr. Linsk in the eyes, he didn't feel safe telling his boss every detail.

"How much longer?" Linsk muttered. His tone had changed. His secretary must have stepped out of the office.

"A few more days," Travis said. "I need to get back for Caroline's birthday. But I need to pay for a few more nights in the motel. And I could use food and gas money for the trip back."

"I'll wire it today," Linsk whispered, then he cleared his

throat. "I'll expect that on my desk the minute you get back." His secretary must have returned.

Maybe she wasn't a spy. Maybe Ricky Aspell wasn't, either. But Travis had to assume he couldn't trust anyone.

He knew truths that someone at the Pentagon was trying to suppress. That sounded like a dangerous position to be in.

"I'll see you in a few days," he told Linsk.

"See that you do," Linsk answered sharply before he hung up the phone.

Travis set the phone on its cradle and stared at it for a moment.

Rosie worked a few days a week as a receptionist in a doctor's office.

But today was one of her days off.

Caroline would already be off to school.

Travis picked up the phone again and dialed.

Rosie's voice was like her smile. It lit up Travis's day. He had called her last night, but it was late by the time he got back from the ACRO meeting. Rosie didn't admit it, but Travis knew he woke her up.

They had only the briefest of conversations. Just long enough to check in and say *I love you.*

Travis wouldn't tell her about the green light, or the alien race of healers. He hadn't told her why he needed to come to Arizona, just that it was another case. He didn't want to get her hopes up. It was hard enough to manage his own. If it worked, he would tell her then. If it didn't, there was no point in telling her anyway.

Travis didn't intend to tell her about the two abductions from the place where he was going tonight. He didn't want to worry her, and that would definitely make her worry.

But he missed her. He missed Caroline. He just wanted to hear what they were doing while he was away.

They spoke for ten minutes. Travis couldn't afford a lengthy long-distance call. But whatever the motel wanted to charge him, it was worth it.

He was meeting Mercedes Fuentes at her shop at three. She was closing early, just for him.

The drive out to Red Rock would take about a half hour. The man they were seeing, Raoul Ortega, started work early in the morning and was usually off by four.

He had no phone, so Mercedes couldn't contact him. They were just going to show up and hope he would talk.

It was the same strategy Mercedes told Travis they would use later tonight, when they drove out to the field where the recent abduction had taken place.

That man had been returned in the morning, just like Raoul Ortega was. But unlike Ortega, the second man remembered nothing.

Travis and Mercedes were going to go to that field. They were just going to show up and hope the Healers would come.

"How often do you communicate with them?" Travis had asked her last night.

"More often lately," Mercedes said. "At least once a week."

"What do they tell you?"

"Things I should know," Mercedes said. "About the world and the human race."

She smiled at Travis then and tilted her head. She gazed at him with her warm brown eyes.

"You seem like a good man," she told him. "I will send out that thought to our friends. Maybe they will hear it and will come to us tomorrow tonight."

When Travis picked up Mercedes at her shop the following afternoon, she said, "I think they heard me. Let's go see."

3

Travis drove his Plymouth Wagon down the dusty road that led to the farm. There was plenty of acreage for agriculture here in the valley between the mountains of Red Rock. The land was still desert, naturally dry, but irrigation allowed crops to grow, and there were livestock grazing on the cultivated late summer grass.

The landscape was mostly brown, not like the rural areas Travis knew in Colorado. But his territory included the entire Four Corners area, Colorado, Utah, Arizona, and New Mexico, so he had spent plenty of time in desert places. They had a beauty of sorts, he had to admit. And apparently alien races felt the same way, or were at least curious about it, because they came to Travis's territory more often than some of the other areas around the country.

One of the criticisms leveled by the Air Force's new UFO-debunking task force was that an inordinate number of alien sightings were made by people out in the boonies, like rural sheriff's deputies and ranchers and farmers.

Dr. Linsk had tried to explain to them the obvious reason why.

"Those are the people outdoors when it's dark," he said. "They either get up early or they're out patrolling at night. So of course more of them are going to see what's going on in the sky than your average person looking out the window of their New York apartment."

Travis could imagine how dark the night sky was out here. No city lights to compete with the stars.

Mercedes said the farm where Raoul Ortega worked came after the feed lot that was about a mile up ahead on their left. As he continued driving the road, Travis could already smell the cattle and manure from this far away. It wasn't the clean animal smell of cows or horses out in the open or even in a barn. This had a rancid, acrid, almost chemical stench, as though thousands of livestock were all crowded together in the belly of a ship.

Travis rolled up his window, but the smell was still coming in. The air was so thick with it, it felt like it had weight.

Mercedes covered her nose with the sleeve of her bright blue blouse. Travis began coughing and he couldn't stop. His lungs had been a problem for the past few years, but he had found ways of keeping them in check. He changed the way he drew in air. Tiny puffs instead of nice full breaths.

And he was careful when he ate and drank not to put too much in his mouth at a time. He didn't want to obstruct his throat and begin choking.

But there was nothing he could do now. The air was thick in his mouth and nose, and his lungs were trying to push it back out.

All of the coughing was making Travis's eyes water. He couldn't see the road clearly enough. He pulled off to the right and opened his door.

He walked in front of the car and bent at the waist. Then he coughed until his breath was heaving.

Mercedes got out of the car and came to his side. She rubbed her hand over his back. It didn't help.

Travis knew from experience it just had to run its course. Every new gasp brought in more of the acrid air. He could see the cows at the feed lot, thousands of them bumping together at lines of trough. They were there to be fattened up before slaughter. Until then they repaid their masters by poisoning the air with the stench of their bodies, their food, and their dung.

Eventually Travis's lungs cleared out and he stumbled back into the car. Mercedes returned to the passenger seat and Travis drove on.

"Now I see," Mercedes said. She stared ahead through the windshield, but she reached over and squeezed Travis's right hand.

He coughed once more, but it was just a quick rattle from his lungs. Then he took his small breaths again and let everything calm down.

They drove past the boundary fence of the feed lot, and then onward another three miles. Travis finally trusted that he could speak without coughing again.

"You see … what?" he asked Mercedes, responding to her comment from minutes ago.

"You are sick. You need their help."

Travis glanced to his right. Mercedes nodded.

Travis's heart bounded through the next few beats. He wasn't sure what to say. Or whether he should say anything at all.

He had already told Mercedes last night about all of his credentials, and that he was an investigator from Colorado State University. There was no point in repeating any of it. No point in lying and saying that was the only reason he came.

"I would be honored if they helped me," Travis said. His heart bounded again and kept up its rapid new pace.

"I will ask them," Mercedes said. "You should have told me last night. I already sent out a message. But maybe they will hear me now."

She closed her eyes and leaned back against her seat. The road was rough. The Plymouth bucked over rocks and dirt. But Mercedes Fuentes breathed deeply and her face looked smooth and placid.

If she was meditating right now, or communicating with aliens, it looked the same as someone napping during a long car ride.

Travis tried harder to avoid the worst of the dips and rocks in the road. Mercedes continued breathing deeply. Travis swallowed down a cough that wanted to bubble to the surface.

Mercedes abruptly opened her eyes and said, "Turn left here." Travis had almost missed it.

He had come to this farm before, but from the opposite direction. He had come the long way around.

Mercedes didn't include names in her Bulletin, so Travis had to find Raoul Ortega on his own. He had done it before, following other leads from her publication. She usually gave enough clues that Travis and the other investigators could track the people down.

But this time it took several days for Travis to learn Ortega's name, and then another few days to find out where he worked. But then when Travis came here, he discovered that Ortega didn't speak English, and even if did, he probably wouldn't want to talk to Travis.

Ortega and his neighbors seemed nervous that Travis had come. He wasn't sure why, and it didn't feel like he could change it.

But he sneaked back the next day and parked on the road, then walked to where he could see Ortega through his binoculars.

That's when he saw the man who had been close to death's door lifting up and tossing around heavy bales of hay.

This was a man who had barely been able to walk, he was in so much pain. But the Healers had taken him and had brought him back well. Travis watched him through his binoculars long enough to confirm it.

Now Travis angled the Plymouth onto the narrower dirt road that led to the farm. He sat up straighter on his seat, anxious about what might happen next.

Mercedes seemed as calm as ever, but she kept her eyes open now. Her meditation was over.

"Did you…?" Travis was afraid to ask if she had been able to contact the Healers on his behalf.

"I told them," Mercedes said. "I don't know if they heard me."

She reached over again and squeezed his right hand. "Don't worry. They are very kind."

The dirt road began curving toward the right. Up ahead Travis could see the farm.

It looked like a substantial operation. Lots of buildings, corrals, and fence line.

"Here," Mercedes pointed, but Travis already knew the way. He turned right onto a spur of road that led to the workers' housing.

The houses were all nearly the same, small wood frame structures with probably two bedrooms, three at most. They looked well cared for. Some of them had little gardens in front.

Brown-skinned children played on the dirt road, but parted to let Travis through. Mothers looked on from front steps and from tending their vegetables and flowers.

Travis didn't see any men. Maybe they were all still working. But then one of them came out of a white painted house and he stood with his arms folded across his chest.

He stared at Travis's car, and Travis stared back. It was Raoul Ortega. Travis pulled to the side of the road and stopped the car.

He looked at Mercedes. She smiled. "I'll go speak to him. Wait here."

Mercedes greeted Ortega and opened her arms for an embrace. Travis saw the man immediately soften and hug her back. They would have met a month ago when Mercedes came here to interview him for the ACRO Bulletin. Mercedes must make friends wherever she went.

The two of them spoke in Spanish for several long minutes. Mercedes gestured toward Travis several times.

At first the man shook his head no a few times. But Mercedes could be persuasive. Raoul Ortega stared into the car at Travis again. But then he shrugged one shoulder and finally nodded.

Mercedes turned toward Travis and smiled. She tilted her head. *Come on in.*

Ortega opened his front door and moved inside. Mercedes followed. Travis got out of the car and did the same.

The house was pretty inside. Obviously a woman's touch. Flowery curtains over all the windows, flowers in a vase on the table, soft colors on the few pieces of furniture.

Ortega offered Mercedes and Travis coffee from the pot sitting on the stove. Mercedes accepted, and so Travis did, too.

The coffee tasted dark and strong, like the brew Mercedes had offered at the ACRO meeting last night. It was far better than what they served at the diner next to Travis's motel.

Ortega set out a loaf of bread and a small saucer with a chunk of butter. He cut a few slices and passed them to his guests.

Travis took that, too. He was starving. He nodded gratefully to Mr. Ortega.

Then Mercedes began speaking again in her rapid and musical Spanish. Ortega nodded. Mercedes turned to Travis.

"He will answer your questions," she said.

Travis's shoulders dropped at least an inch. He bowed his head in a sign of respect.

Then he asked Mr. Ortega to tell him everything that happened, from the beginning, leaving nothing out.

It was much as Mercedes Fuentes had already told Travis last night. There were a few new details, and Travis pulled a small spiral-bound notebook out of his pocket to write them down.

He was dressed the way he usually did for field work: jeans, sturdy cotton shirt, hiking boots. The first time he tried to talk to Mr. Ortega he had been wearing clothes like he wore last night. He meant to look like a professional scientist, but he probably looked like someone from the government instead.

When Mr. Ortega got to the part where he started describing the alien Healers, Travis set down his notebook and just listened. There was always a lapse between Ortega's speaking and then Mercedes translating it, and Travis wanted to pay close attention to both.

Mr. Ortega used his hands when he spoke. He drew pictures in the air. Travis wanted to see how he drew pictures of the aliens.

Tall. Ortega held his hand about three inches above his own head. He looked to be about Travis's height, average.

Mr. Ortega pointed to his fingers when he described the webbing on the aliens' hands. Apparently it began above the first knuckle.

In response to Travis's question about the shape of the aliens' bodies, Mr. Ortega motioned his hands down in a straight line, no curves at all.

"But women," Travis said, then he waited for Mercedes to translate.

"*Si mujeres,*" Ortega answered.

"Yes, women," Mercedes translated. Then she asked Ortega a question of her own. She told Travis, "He thought they were naked, but he couldn't see any breasts or…" She gestured toward her lap.

"Then why does he think they were women?" Travis asked.

Mercedes translated the question and then the answer.

"Because they had pretty faces and long silver hair."

Mr. Ortega spoke again. Mercedes added to his answer.

"And when he heard their voices speaking inside his ears, they were women's voices, not men's."

"Is that what you hear, too?" Travis asked. "When you communicate with them?"

"Yes, most definitely," Mercedes answered.

The interview lasted a little over an hour. Travis ate another slice of bread and had a second cup of the rich dark coffee.

Then the front door opened and Mr. Ortega's wife and teenage daughter returned from wherever they had been. Mr. Ortega stood up from his table, signaling it was time for his guests to leave.

Mercedes brought out the map Travis had given her. She spread it over a section of the table. She spoke in rapid Spanish, trying to get this one more piece of information.

"*Sí,*" said Mr. Ortega, confirming the spot where he was taken up in the ship. He had already told Mercedes the location when she wrote her report for the ACRO Bulletin, but Travis needed to make sure. Both for his official investigation, and for himself.

"*Gracias,*" he told Raoul Ortega, the healthy, vital man. Travis looked at the wife and daughter who almost lost their husband and father.

He thought of Rosie and Caroline. Of Caroline as a teenager in a few years. Travis wanted to live long enough to see her grown.

He smiled at Mr. Ortega's family, and Mercedes spoke briefly to them both, then Mercedes led the way back to the car.

Travis could feel the eyes of the neighbors and the little children playing on the road. He started up the Plymouth and drove out of sight.

When they were alone again on the road leading away from the farm, Travis let out a breath and then smiled at Mercedes.

"I couldn't have done it without you," he said.

"*De nada,*" Mercedes answered.

"I'll take you home now," Travis said.

"No, you will not."

So he bought her dinner, and then they returned. Together.

By the light of a flashlight, Mercedes directed him from the map. Travis drove to where Mr. Ortega was taken.

It was about a mile from where the second abductee

woke up yesterday morning. Whether he was taken from that same spot, the second man couldn't say.

Travis pulled the Plymouth onto the side of the dirt road. He sat for a moment, not ready to get out.

"Are you afraid?" Mercedes asked.

"Yes," he admitted.

"Our friends are kind," Mercedes assured him. "You will see."

The nighttime temperature felt cool, as though autumn might be coming here after all. A light breeze blew across the field and made the air smell clean again. A half moon lit up the sky as much as it could. The stars winkled brightly against the velvety black.

Travis brought his flashlight from the glove compartment and aimed its beam onto the bumpy surface of the field. Mercedes stumbled once, and Travis caught her arm.

"How sick are you?" Mercedes asked him. She put her hand over his. She held on until he answered.

"I might have another year," Travis said. "I'm not sure. Some of my colleagues have died. Most of us are sick."

Mercedes let go of his hand and walked on. She asked him, "Do you believe?"

Travis thought about it before answering. "I believe a lot of things. I've seen a lot of things. So yes, I believe this, too."

"Good," Mercedes answered. "Because there are my friends." She pointed straight ahead into the distance.

Travis strained to see. There were no flashing or colored lights. Nothing like he expected to find.

He played the beam of his flashlight higher, up off the ground. He could see someone walking toward them.

"Go with them now," Mercedes said. "I will take your car and come back for you in the morning."

Travis's heart sped. It couldn't happen this easily or this soon. He thought this would be different. He thought it would be harder.

Mercedes's hand was warm as it reached down and squeezed his own.

The figure walking toward them was almost here.

Mercedes let go of Travis and pressed her palms together and bowed low at the waist. Then she held out her right palm toward Travis as though introducing him.

Travis stared at the being in front of them. Raoul Ortega was right, the alien was beautiful. Her face looked small and delicate, everything feminine and in perfect proportion, except for her eyes. Mr. Ortega was right, they were bigger than human eyes, maybe even twice as wide. But they weren't grotesque or frightening, just something that drew his gaze. Strange, but also beautiful.

The three of them stood together on the field for a silent space of time. Then Travis knew he was ready to go.

He handed Mercedes his flashlight. He doubted he would need it anymore. There was a glow coming from the alien's body, bright enough for Travis to see by.

Mercedes hugged him quickly. She whispered, *"Buena suerte," Good luck,* and added, "I'll come look for you in the morning."

Then Mercedes pivoted in the dirt and walked away.

And Travis Baird went up.

HIDEAWAY

1

The snow fell wet and heavy, numbing Marnie's fingers. It slapped against her face and stung her straining, bloodshot green eyes.

Marnie had flown through snow before. And rain, and sleet, and winds so strong they whipped her all over the sky and made her wonder if this would be the day she fell.

She was taller than average, slim, with tight muscular arms like a climber, but legs that were used to doing less of the work. At most, they helped her get a running start so she could take off and pump her arms hard until she was airborne, the way people did in their flying dreams. The way Marnie used to dream of, too, back before everything went wrong.

She wore a custom-made one-piece matte gray flight suit, skin tight, that covered her from head to foot. The only two exposed areas were the central circle of her burning cold face and the tips of her hands outside the tight sleeves that covered her to her knuckles.

She had tucked her short brown hair into the hood of the flight suit, like a swimmer tucking her hair into a swim cap. She carried nothing. No extra clothing, no money, no food or water. This was not the first time she had to travel so light. Marnie Stemple was twenty-eight, used to being alone, used to running away at a moment's notice. Used to flight.

The wind bullied the snow sideways, making it fall horizontally to the left. It tried to shove Marnie along with it. But like a bird she adjusted herself without consciously making the effort. She angled her arms, her body, her legs, like she had done thousands of times before.

Visibility was nearly nil. All around her were the snow-laden slopes of the Wasatch Mountain Range in Utah, but Marnie doubted she would crash into any of them. That, too, was a feature of her condition. A kind of spatial awareness she assumed birds had as well, telling them when something solid was close by.

Late afternoon sunlight glowed weakly through the screen of tumbling white. It might be around four o'clock already, which meant sunset was less than an hour away. Still time enough to keep going, to put distance between herself and the Factory, to get somewhere dark and lonely where she could hide and think about what to do next.

Of course they were looking for her. From now on, people would always be looking. Marnie's days of anonymity were over. Had been ever since her slimy co-worker with the Hitler haircut turned her in to the feds.

For what crime? Not a crime, but sheer nosiness. And

probably shock, and maybe even worry, as if seeing a woman flying under her own power, gliding through the air like she could swim through it, were a threat to humanity somehow.

Marnie was used to leaving at the first flash of a potential threat. Over the past eleven years, her instinct for danger had grown ever and ever sharper.

She had been on the run since she was seventeen years old, since shortly after her mother died. Marnie had a good mind and some employable skills—restaurant server, administrative assistant, bookkeeper—and could settle in a new place quickly. New name, same story of an abusive husband who might still be looking for her, so let's not use my social security number or do any paperwork. Please pay me in cash.

She would construct a new life for a few weeks or months, hoping maybe this time she would be safe. But always ready to flee at the first sign that she wasn't.

Sometimes, if she had enough warning, she managed to escape with a lightweight backpack holding a few of her latest possessions, but today wasn't the first time she had left with only the clothes on her back.

At least this time the clothes were good. Superior to anything she'd ever worn. Warm and streamlined, the special flight suit had been made just for her. A gift from Major Fritz Zimholt, the grandfatherly man who offered both Marnie and her friend Alice Kern sanctuary inside the Factory, his hidden facility beneath one of these snow-covered mountains.

But not so grandfatherly after all. Major Zimholt was an

opportunist, just like everybody else. Marnie should know by now that everything came with a cost.

She had overheard enough of a conversation between Major Zimholt and one of his pilots to know they had plans for Marnie. Something they intended to make her do. And they planned to lie to her about it, to try to trick her into whatever it was.

Marnie's mother had warned her long ago that people would hunt Marnie for her gift. The government, the military, some other group with enough money and power. And once they got ahold of her, who knew what experiments they would do. Marnie was one of a kind. A human who had learned how to fly. What people wouldn't give to learn that secret for themselves. What they wouldn't do to take it.

So she left with just the clothes on her back, although those clothes now posed a problem. Warm, streamlined, yes. And made from a special fabric that rendered Marnie invisible to the naked eye as she flew.

But not, Marnie knew now, invisible to Major Zimholt's pilots.

Sharman Hix, the young black woman who was the pilot Marnie overheard scheming with Major Zimholt, had let slip that she and all the other pilots could see Marnie from inside their aircrafts.

"We're made of the same thing," Sharman told her. The same material in Marnie's flight suit coated the outside of the small experimental pods the pilots flew. Even though the pods were invisible to anyone searching for them in the skies, the pilots could all see each other from inside their crafts. "I can see you, too," Sharman said.

Which meant that someone might be following Marnie right now, despite the blinding storm. Warm and cozy inside one of the pods, just hanging back and watching where Marnie went.

She had only two choices that she could see. Either ditch the flight suit and fly in just her undergarments for a while to try to lose any tail in the storm.

Or keep the warm, insulating suit—which, as Marnie flew on through the wet and freezing air, felt like the smarter and saner choice—but find shelter somewhere where she could hide for the night.

But that meant shaking off anyone following her first.

Marnie flew on and thought. She hoped to find a solution before the last of the daylight left.

2

"She's been gone too long," Alice Kern told Major Zimholt. "She'll freeze to death out there."

Marnie had been missing for over two hours. And Alice had only known about it for the past twenty minutes.

She'd been down in the belly of the Factory, in one of the computer rooms, scrolling from one innocuous document to the next. Following the slightest trail of bread crumbs. Wielding her innate talent for patient and meticulous research.

Somewhere in those files she would find answers. Answers to who was trying to kill her. And who had murdered her parents.

Alice was twenty-six, small and dark like her Filipino mother, with long brown hair and calm, observant eyes. Because of her size, people often assumed Alice was younger than she was. Maybe a college student. Maybe even high school.

They underestimated her intelligence and her strength. Alice took advantage of that whenever she could. She was a junior analyst with the Agency, a governmental entity with an intentionally non-descript name that had tentacles into more places than her superiors openly admitted. Alice was also a third-degree black belt and skilled with weapons of various kinds.

In the past month, she had killed two men who had been sent to kill her. Alice still didn't know who sent them or why.

But Major Zimholt had promised her answers, and Alice was at the Factory to collect.

She had come here on two conditions: unlimited access to Major Zimholt's computer files, and protection for both her and Marnie.

But now Marnie was gone. And Alice had no idea where or why. She thought Marnie was happy here, free to fly whenever she wanted, no demands put on her by anyone.

But obviously sometime in the past several hours, something had gone wrong.

"Who saw her last?" Alice asked Major Zimholt.

The two of them stood inside the Factory's cavernous hangar hidden under the surface of a mountain. The space felt huge, wide and long and tall like an indoor stadium, and smelled faintly of damp concrete.

Major Zimholt stood tall and dignified, fit for a man in his mid-seventies. He was bald with a rim of short white hair on the lower half of his scalp. His white beard was neatly-trimmed.

He looked like one of the rich businessmen who flew in

on private jets to ski at Deer Valley or Snowbird or one of the other nearby resorts. He wore dark gray slacks and a well-made navy blue wool sweater. Expensive watch, expensive boots. Alice could see the remnants of snow on those boots, which told her that Major Zimholt must have gone up the metal stairs from the hangar, up topside where he could examine the storm for himself.

"One of my pilots let Marnie do a trial flight in her pod," Major Zimholt answered. "Sharman Hix. She's one of my best. She said Marnie liked it and flew well. No issue there."

"But *some* issue," Alice said, keeping her voice as neutral as she could. She didn't much care for Sharman Hix, even though they still hadn't been formally introduced. Something about the young pilot rubbed her the wrong way.

"Sharman has a team out there right now," said Major Zimholt. "They've been looking for Marnie for a while. The conditions are making things difficult. But they'll find her. Don't worry."

Alice did worry. About all of it. If Marnie was out there now, fleeing somewhere in this storm, there had to be a reason. There had to be some immediate and dangerous threat. Otherwise Alice didn't believe her friend would have left her. They had come too far together by now.

"Don't you have radar or something?" Alice asked. "Some way of seeing her?"

"I'm sending out two more pilots right now," said Major Zimholt. "Trust me, one way or another we'll find her."

If he was that confident, why had he sent anyone to tell Alice? Why now? Wouldn't it be better to find Marnie first and confess it to Alice later?

Major Zimholt watched one of the pods rise smoothly from the floor of the hangar. It was a small wingless sphere that had room enough for only the pilot. And not a large pilot, either. Alice knew from talking to one of them that it was best if they were built like jockeys.

The pod continued to rise like a carbonated bubble. Then a hole opened in the ceiling and the pod popped through.

Major Zimholt crossed his arms over his chest and watched the second pod move into position.

"Did Marnie … say anything to you?" he asked. "Last night or this morning?"

So that was the reason he sent for her. They didn't have a clue where Marnie was. They needed Alice's help.

"No. She's been happy here," Alice said. "I thought."

Major Zimholt nodded. His slim black wristwatch buzzed once. He looked down and read some incoming communication. Then he gave Alice his attention again.

"You know her," he said. "Where would she go?"

Alice sighed. "Anywhere. She just runs. That's how she's stayed free all these years. She's good at it."

Alice didn't want to say it, because she didn't want to believe it. But she'd trained herself over the past few years to face up to hard, ugly truths.

She thought that she and Marnie were friends now. She assumed that Marnie would have come to her if something was wrong.

Certainly come to her before just taking off and leaving. But maybe Alice had misread the whole situation.

"Whatever scared her off," Alice said, "that might be it for us. She might be gone forever."

Major Zimholt didn't seem ready to accept that. "We'll keep looking. We'll find her."

3

Sharman Hix wrestled to control her pod in the wild currents of the storm. The craft didn't want to do the things she asked it. It kept throwing her off her line.

"I have to find Marnie," she told the craft out loud. She wasn't calm enough to say it only with her mind. But the pod bucked through the air again, then spiraled on a path of its own.

Sharman was the best pilot in the Factory's program and she was failing.

The pods weren't like regular aircraft, even the experimental ones. They might look like spaceships, but they weren't. Not really. They were more like horses. They were alive. They had emotions. They had opinions.

Who made them, how Major Zimholt got hold of them, Sharman still didn't know.

She wore a lighted band around her head—they called it a head harness—that helped her communicate telepathically

47

with the pod. There were no visible controls inside the craft. No displays or dials or levers. Just the pilot's chair, which molded itself to whoever sat there.

Although all the other pilots wore their soft black boots when they flew, Sharman preferred to ride barefoot so she could touch her bare skin against the skin of the pod. When she slid her arms on top of the arm rests, she liked to press her fingers into the joints at the end. She molded to the pod while it molded to her. Then Sharman flew her craft as much by feel as by thought.

This personal connection with the pod wasn't really something she could teach anyone else. You either got it or you didn't. She was in charge of selecting and training all the new pilots in the program. She could tell within the first ten or fifteen minutes whether a pilot belonged.

This team out with her now were the top of the line. But from what she could see through the clear dome that made up the top half of her pod, all of the rest of them were failing, too. Some of their pods were crawling so slowly through the blowing snow, it was like they were on the ground, trying to plow through snow drifts. Other pods were bucking and swirling like Sharman's, getting churned around by the wind like pinecones trapped in a whirlpool.

In her six years of flying for Major Zimholt, Sharman had seen too many pilots crash. One moment a pod was airborne, and the next it slammed into the side of the mountain and exploded into oblivion.

Sharman had no intention of losing anyone on her team. And no intention of dying out here herself.

All of this was her fault. She knew it. She was the reason

Marnie Stemple fled. But Sharman was in charge, and she refused to let any of this get worse.

She had gone over her last conversation with Marnie Stemple more than a dozen times in her mind. I said this, she said that.

And then suddenly Sharman knew what she'd done wrong. Dammit. Stupid, beginner mistake.

Earlier today, she had enticed Marnie into trying one of the pods for herself. From everything Sharman knew, Marnie should be a natural.

She could already make her body fly like her own personal aircraft. Sharman was just adding a bubble around her, and encouraging Marnie to fly a different way.

But Sharman had given Marnie one of the head harnesses, and kept her own for herself. Training wheels, she told Marnie.

Sharman wanted to be backup, to talk to the ship if she saw that Marnie couldn't control it.

But it meant that Marnie must have heard Sharman's conversation with Major Zimholt, talking behind Marnie's back.

Talking about their plan to convince Marnie to start teaching all the pilots in the program. Marnie knew about flying from the inside of her body out. She had experience that Sharman and others didn't have, no matter how many flights they had taken.

Marnie's mind was already one with her flying body. She could teach the pilots how to be one with their pods.

It didn't sound bad to Sharman. She assumed Marnie would be flattered that they asked.

But there must have been something about that conversation that spooked her. Sharman simply forgot she could overhear.

So now that crazy flier was somewhere out in this storm. And as much as Sharman wanted to find her and bring her back, she couldn't keep searching at the risk of her team.

She spoke out loud inside the pod, even though she could have silently thought it. Her head harness allowed her to communicate mind to mind with the other pilots.

"Leader, leader," Sharman said, identifying herself. "Head back. This storm is too much. If it clears up later, some of us may come out again tonight. Over."

She hated to admit defeat. *Hated* it. But being stubborn and foolish was worse. Major Zimholt had put her in charge for a reason.

Two years ago, when Sharman was twenty-two, Major Zimholt named her Senior Pilot First Class. She was the youngest pilot in the program to earn that distinction.

Not long afterward, Sharman had a heart-to-heart with the Major. She told him she was sick of seeing people die who didn't belong in the pods to begin with. Good pilots, all of them, but not good with these temperamental craft. And they had paid for it with their lives.

Major Zimholt made Sharman leader of the pilot program. She was mindful of his trust. And determined never to let him down.

So as she broke the bad news to him that they were heading back now without Marnie, Sharman could imagine Major Zimholt seeing her update on the face of his black watch and frowning at what he read.

Sharman watched her original team and the two newest additions Major Zimholt had sent out as they all turned their pods for home. Sharman could always feel her own pod responding whenever she did that, like a horse eager to return to the stable.

But Sharman didn't turn her pod back right away. There was still the slightest bit of daylight left. The storm was still pounding her from every which way, but Sharman was better than the other pilots. She still had a shot at coming out the hero.

Maybe it was pride. She'd own that. But it was also duty. And disgust. She was the one who screwed up. She was the one who had to fix this.

"Come on, pal," she said to her pod. "Just give me a little more. Let's go find our girl."

She'd give it another half hour. Maybe a little more. She wouldn't head back until dead dark. The pod reluctantly pushed through the storm. Sharman Hix flew on.

4

Marnie could feel herself tiring. She had already flown for several hours this morning, simply for the joy of it, before this hurried and difficult break toward freedom.

Even though the sun had been just a glow behind the smothering snow for a while, now Marnie could barely see anything except the movement of her own arms whenever she stroked them out in front of her.

When she was tired like this, she resorted to breast stroke. Back when she was on a swim team when she was a child, her coach said that breast stroke was a lazy stroke. Not powerful and dynamic like freestyle or butterfly.

Right now lazy was the best that Marnie could do.

She had to stop soon. To rest and find shelter. The last few glimmers of daylight were dying.

Marnie glanced behind her, wondering if she could see any of the pods that might be following her. But the storm was still too thick. The wind too severe. She faced forward again and kept on breast stroking through the air.

She could feel her arms giving up. This was the most dangerous time. She had fallen before, even quite recently when she tried hovering in the air for too long.

Marnie closed her eyes. She was tired of the wind and the snow. Tired of running. Tired, for now, of flying.

She let herself drift a few moments. Let the storm have its way.

But then her eyes flew open again and she quickly beat her arms with as much strength as she could.

She could see the shape of a snow-covered slope suddenly looming right in front of her.

Marnie's heart hammered hard. She panted with fear and exertion. She hauled herself back toward the right, stroke by arduous stroke, like a swimmer fighting the ocean's storm-tossed waves.

At last she was back in safe air. Marnie doubted that she would have hit the mountain head on, but she didn't trust herself to fly safely anymore. She had to get down. Now.

She strained to see what was there on the slope she just dodged. Everything was coated in white.

But there were boulders sticking out of the snow here and there, and trees, plenty of trees.

The rocks were good for landing, but they offered no shelter from the wind. So a tree would have to do for now.

Marnie aimed for the closest blue spruce. It stood like a giant shadow in the dark. There were bare aspens and other fir and spruce all around, but she chose one with a thick enough trunk that she could hide behind it, out of the wind and out of sight of any pods.

If they were tracking her based on body heat, maybe they would still find her no matter what.

But Marnie was done. She landed at the base of the spruce and sank up to her knees in snow. She moved behind the trunk to hide, then felt her legs give way before she collapsed in total exhaustion.

She must have slept. Although it felt closer to being unconscious. Like she was back in the infirmary, drugged.

When she awoke again it was still nighttime. The storm still raged and blew outside.

But Marnie was inside. Someplace light and dry and warm.

Somebody had moved her. Rescued her.

Or captured her.

5

Marnie lay as still as possible and pretended to be asleep. She kept her eyes open only a fraction, in case she was being watched. She couldn't hear anyone near her, no shifting feet or rustling clothes, but she couldn't trust that. She couldn't trust anything.

She lay on her back, on some kind of soft surface. There was something warm on top of her, maybe a blanket. It looked white. Like thick white wool. But it smelled like something else. Like freshly-cut green grass.

Marnie moderated her breath. She had to stay quiet. How would she sound if she were still sleeping? Slow and steady. Calm.

Above her she could see the dark night sky still swirling with snow. The ceiling must be made of glass.

This wasn't the Factory. Or at least no room she had seen there so far. If Major Zimholt or Sharman Hix or someone from there had brought Marnie back, wouldn't they take her to her own room? Wouldn't Alice be here right now?

Not the Factory. Someplace else.

Marnie saw movement from the corner of her left eye. She dropped her lids and tried to stay still.

I see you, came a woman's voice inside her head. *You are safe here. I promise.*

Marnie risked opening her eyes. If the woman was lying, if Marnie was in danger, it would be better to know. Better to have some kind of plan. Look for a way to escape.

Marnie sat up. The white blanket around her shoulders draped down to her lap. There was a similar thick white blanket beneath her, cushioning her from what looked like a hard, charcoal-colored floor.

Marnie was still wearing her gray flight suit, but someone had pushed back the hood from the top of her head. Her short brown hair hung free.

Marnie was free, too. No binding around her wrists or ankles. At least that was something.

The room was small, no larger than a hotel room or Marnie's room back at the Factory. All the walls were made of glass. Marnie could see snow beating against the exterior, but the walls kept the sound of the wind and storm from reaching them inside. The room was as quiet as if they were underwater.

A woman stood a few feet away. She smiled at Marnie. *Are you thirsty?*

The woman's lips never moved. Marnie could hear her voice inside her mind. Marnie nodded, numbly.

She was thirsty. Painfully so. She hadn't had anything to

drink since back at the Factory this morning. If it was this morning. Marnie had no idea how much time had passed since she collapsed in the snow behind the giant spruce tree.

But her thirst was a small matter compared to the sight before her eyes.

The woman was slim, like Marnie, maybe slightly taller, with long silver hair that reached down to her lower back. The strands of her hair looked like the most delicate silver filament, too fine and lightweight to see one single strand at a time.

Her skin had a pale green tint, almost imperceptible. Marnie blinked and looked harder to make sure. The woman wore a long, flowing garment shaped like a poncho. It, too, was a light pale green. The sides of it hung down like long, loose sleeves, covering her arms to the wrists. Then it continued downward, draping loosely all the way to her ankles. It had no real shape or design, but looked as though she had taken a large piece of fabric and simply cut a hole in the center for her head.

Besides a few snowy-white blankets on the floor, there were only two other items in the room. One was an elegant silver pitcher made in the shape of a swan, with its open beak serving as the lip from which to pour. The handle was hidden between two silver wings that looked poised to open wider and carry the pitcher away. Whoever made it was a true artist.

Next to it sat a silver cup, oddly shaped, like two eggs attached together and then stretched to twice their height and chopped off at the top to make a level rim. Both the cup and the pitcher seemed to rest in midair, about the height of the woman's waist.

Marnie looked harder. The lighting in the room didn't offer any shadows to give her perspective, but she suspected that the cup and pitcher sat on some kind of transparent surface she couldn't see.

The woman lifted the pitcher. It seemed to have very little weight. She poured liquid from it into the silver cup. She set down the pitcher on the transparent ledge and cradled the cup in both of her hands. She carried it to Marnie, who still sat up wrapped in soft white blankets.

The woman was graceful, beautiful to watch. She moved with an erect and regal bearing like a dancer. Or a queen.

She knelt beside Marnie and held out the cup to her with both hands.

Marnie saw webbing between all of the woman's fingers.

She looked down at the woman's bare feet peeking out from beneath the flowing green garment. Same webbing between her toes.

A thrill traveled through Marnie's nerves. She knew what this woman was. An alien. A being from another world. She had to be. There was no other explanation.

Major Zimholt had said that the Factory specialized in alien technology. Marnie's flight suit, that made her invisible as she flew—that stopped a bullet that should have pierced her chest—was a product of alien tech. So were the pods that responded to thoughts, not physical controls. The beam of light that Dr. Caroline Baird had used to heal Major Zimholt's arm and Marnie's broken ankle—all of them were alien.

It wasn't just a story. It wasn't just history, something that had happened back in the 1940s when a UFO crashed in Roswell, New Mexico.

It was here, now. Present.

Alice had been skeptical, but not Marnie. Marnie had seen strange things in her life. She *was* a strange thing. Her mother had been, too.

Marnie smiled. She couldn't help it. She had felt like an alien since she was sixteen. Like an *other*. A freak.

She wasn't alone in this universe.

The woman smiled back. She gazed at Marnie with eyes that looked as though they were made of liquid silver. They were oval rather than round, shaped the way Marnie used to draw eyes when she was a little girl. A curving line on top, like an eyebrow, and a matching curved line underneath. They were wider than a human eye, with small black pupils in the center.

The woman had pale green eyelids, but no lashes or eyebrows. The rest of her features looked human: small, straight nose, a wide mouth with two pale green lips, rounded green ears that Marnie could see peeking out from the woman's fine silver hair.

She was beautiful. Graceful and fluid in her movements. Her skin was the color of something fresh growing in spring. The gaze from her silver eyes looked kind. Her smile was gentle, and almost … motherly. Marnie felt safe in this woman's—this alien woman's—presence. Safe and calm and welcome.

The words came into Marnie's mind. *I am Hoala. I know you are Marnie. How do you feel? Are you well?*

Marnie nodded. "But thirsty," she said, looking down at the silver cup Hoala held between her webbed hands.

Hoala offered her the cup and Marnie took it and gratefully drank. She wasn't sure what the liquid was. Not pure water. It was slightly thicker than that and had a sweet and piney taste. It felt refreshing as it slid down Marnie's dry throat. And just that one portion quenched her thirst as well as a gallon. Marnie handed the cup back empty.

Rest now, Hoala said. But Marnie didn't want to rest. She had too many questions. This wasn't the time to sleep.

But a drowsiness overcame her, even though Marnie fought it. She wondered if the drink had been drugged. Or maybe it was just the effect of the alien's suggestion. Some kind of mind control.

Whatever the cause, Marnie did sleep. The next time she opened her eyes, the pale light of dawn bathed the room.

Marnie needed a moment to reorient herself. She stared up at the glass ceiling. It angled at the top, like the tip of a pyramid. Beyond it Marnie could see plump white clouds floating in a bright blue sky. The storm had passed sometime during the night, leaving a thick new layer of snow on the mountain peaks all around.

Marnie sat up. The grass-scented white blanket bunched onto her lap. The woman, Hoala, was still here. She sat on a blanket of her own, staring out across the landscape. But at the sound of Marnie moving, Hoala turned around with a smile and faced her.

Now are you well?

Marnie realized she was. The extra sleep had seeped into her bones. She felt better than she had in memory. She could picture even her blood cells looking healthy and iron-rich and plump.

She stared past Hoala to the view outside. From where she sat, Marnie imagined they were inside some kind of spaceship, floating in mid-air.

The entire structure was made of glass. There were no windows or doors, only transparent windows rising from the floor and meeting in a triangular peak at the top.

Marnie looked at the floor. What she mistook last night for some kind of hard, charcoal surface was actually more of the glass. Beneath it was solid gray rock.

"Not a spaceship," Marnie said.

No. Come see.

Marnie joined Hoala to gaze out of the nearest wall.

Miles of forest stretched out beneath them. The fir and spruce trees held pillows of snow on their upper boughs. All around were the white peaks of the Wasatch mountains. This glass shelter stood at the same height as many of them.

In the distance, toward her right, Marnie could see a small private airport. She knew the place well. Beneath it, hidden from searching eyes, was the secret concrete warren of the Factory.

Marnie couldn't help her disappointment. She hadn't flown nearly as far from the Factory as she thought. All that effort, and only half the distance she expected.

But her misperception bothered her more. She had always relied on her own internal navigation to keep her safe. How had she gotten it so wrong this time? She felt an anxious flutter in her nerves.

This time Hoala spoke out loud. The sound was soft and

beautiful, pleasant to Marnie's ears. "You did fly far," she said. "I found you sleeping in the forest under a tree, a great distance away. I brought you back with me last night."

"How?" Marnie asked. "How did you carry me?"

Hoala smiled. "I will show you some day. But now I think we should fly."

Marnie gazed at her in wonder. Not only because Hoala understood what Marnie needed most, but because of the *we. We should fly.*

The need had been building higher and higher for the past several minutes. It had been hours since Marnie last flew. The compulsion itched at the nerves all along her spine and up and down her arms to the tips of her fingers.

"How?" Marnie asked. She looked around her at the solid enclosure. There were no openings. No way to enter or escape.

Hoala passed her webbed hand through the air, as though wiping a smudge away from the glass.

And then the glass walls disappeared. The morning wind came whipping against Marnie's cheeks. The air was cold. It felt wonderfully fresh and alive. It blustered Marnie's hair into her eyes. She raised the hood of her flight suit and tucked her hair inside.

Hoala's long silver hair blew wild and free. She closed her silvery eyes and breathed in deeply.

Looking down at the snow-laden mountain slope beneath them, Marnie understood now where she and Hola had been since last night.

Somehow, improbably, they had been inside the very tip of the mountain, up where the rock was hollow.

Not hollow, Hoala said. The wind was too loud to bother with speech. She spoke inside Marnie's mind. *I will show you later. Come.*

Hoala cast off her pale green covering, revealing her bare pale green skin underneath. Her body was flat and smooth from her chest to her groin, like the dolls Marnie used to have. If she hadn't already assumed Hoala was a woman, she wouldn't know it now from Hoala's naked frame.

Hoala stood on the brink of the mountain peak and opened her arms wide to her sides.

Marnie saw now what Hoala's clothing had concealed. She had pale green webbing underneath her arms, like the flesh-covered wings of a bat.

Hoala pitched herself forward and fell through the air. Then she beat her wings and rose again.

Marnie forgot her own insistent compulsion for the moment. She just wanted to stand where she was and watch Hoala fly. It wasn't how Marnie did it at all. Hoala was elegant and languid, with her winged arms open wide to the cold wind. She seemed to soar along effortlessly. She barely had to stroke the air to maintain altitude. She glided wherever she wanted with just the smallest angling of her arms, out over the tops of the forest, down toward the icy stream, back up to the trees. Her long silver hair flowed behind her like a ribbon of pale gray smoke. Her green skin looked flawless and otherworldly in the soft morning light and seemed darker now in contrast to the snow on the surrounding peaks.

Something clicked in Marnie. Something she understood for the very first time. She knew she lacked all of

Hoala's grace, but even so, she realized now what it must have been like for her mother to see Marnie fly that very first time. To take off running in the Alaskan snow, beating her arms against the air, and then rising away from the earth.

Marnie's mother had been ecstatic at first that her ritual finally worked. But now Marnie could also understand the depth of her mother's envy.

To see something impossible. Both impossible and beautiful. Marnie watched Hoala fly and felt the pang in her own heart. For so long, Marnie had thought of her condition, her compulsion, as nothing but a burden. It had brought her more pain than pleasure. And yet seeing someone else fly—and doing it so much better than Marnie ever could—filled her with a kind of longing, a wish that might have wings and grace like that.

Marnie wasn't content anymore to just watch and wait. She needed to jump in and join. Even if her own way of flying looked primitive and awkward next to Hoala's. Marnie felt a stirring to want to fly simply for the beauty of flying.

She launched herself from the mountain peak. She beat her wingless arms against the air. She felt like a fledgling trying to follow its mother. But Marnie found her rhythm and her stroke again, and sailed over the forest to catch up with Hoala.

The two of them rode the currents of air together. Marnie always behind, always watching in awe.

As the morning sun crowned the distant peaks, Marnie felt a joy she hadn't felt since her first flight.

This was what she could do. This was the gift her mother gave her. Even if everything turned terrible and tragic after.

There had been that night, that first night, when Marnie was sixteen, and her mother finally found the magic she so desperately sought. A night of utter joy.

Even knowing everything that happened after that, would Marnie want this feeling again? Even if it only lasted the space of a single flight? It was a rapture unlike anything else. Anyone in the world would beg for it, even for five minutes.

But Marnie knew better. This feeling of flight was like a drug. Like the fleeting and deadly lure of the perfect high. Marnie wasn't sixteen anymore. She knew the price both she and her mother had paid. Their afflictions had cost them too much.

Hoala must have heard all of it. All of Marnie's dark and sorrowful thoughts. She drew down toward the forest, to the highest tree.

She caught up a branch near the top and waited for Marnie there. The towering spruce swayed in the wind.

Marnie didn't land on trees. She didn't trust them to hold her weight. And they were uncomfortable. Spiky and sharp.

But Hoala passed her hand across her feet and created a transparent platform there. Marnie landed beside her, safe and secure.

Then Hoala swept her webbed hands to her sides and over her head, building transparent walls to surround them. The structure didn't need a ceiling. The walls met in an angle at the top, like a pyramid.

The shelter was warm. Quiet. Out of the wind. Marnie

panted with exertion. Her heart beat too fast. Just thinking of her mother again had that effect. Especially today, on the anniversary of that one night that had seemed so perfect. Before everything started going wrong.

Marnie lost her mother that night. She just didn't realize it until later.

Hoala had been standing silently beside her while Marnie's thoughts spun out deeper into darkness. But Marnie forced herself back to the present. She had learned not to let herself be trapped in the past. There was nothing but pain there.

She turned to Hoala and saw the alien gazing at her with sympathetic eyes. The pain on her pale green face mirrored Marnie's.

Hoala reached out her webbed fingers and clasped Marnie's. Hoala's skin was dry and warm and soft.

You are brave, Hoala told her.

Marnie let out a soft cry of surprise. And grief. Grief she normally kept in check.

Marnie bowed her head and kept her lips pressed together. If she allowed the tears to come, they wouldn't stop.

She took a few deep breaths and steadied herself. When she had control again, she cleared her throat.

"How do you do this?" she asked Hoala, gesturing to the shelter around them. "How ... is it something I can learn?"

Marnie wouldn't even consider it possible if not for what Major Zimholt had told her before. That people had found ways to reverse-engineer the alien technology left behind.

It would make Marnie's life so much easier if she could

build her own nest wherever she went. Someplace sheltered and out of the weather.

"Can anyone see us up here?" she thought to ask.

Hoala smiled and shook her head.

Someplace sheltered and *invisible*. Was it too much to ask? Marnie waited and hoped for Hoala's answer.

Hoala turned to her left and looked to the sky. There were several gray dots visible in the distance.

Pods. At least five of them.

"Your friends search for you," Hoala said in her soft and soothing voice.

Marnie wasn't surprised that Hoala could see them. The pods were covered in the same material as in Marnie's flight suit, but Hoala had been able to see her, too, flying through the storm.

Your friends search for you.

They weren't Marnie's friends. Major Zimholt had sent them out to look for her because he wanted something from her.

Something he was going to lie about to trick Marnie to give it.

Marnie felt a hard pit in her stomach. She didn't want to be found. She didn't want to go back.

What she wanted was to stay with Hoala. What she wanted was to find a home. Some kind of safe, permanent hideaway where no one tried to force Marnie to do what-ever they wanted.

She would miss Alice, but that was all. It had been nice for a time to have a friend, but right now Marnie wanted her freedom more.

"Please," she told Hoala. "Let me stay with you. Please."

Hoala smiled sadly and shook her head.

Marnie pressed her lips together again. She would control herself. She wouldn't fall apart.

"But I will teach you," Hoala said. "Just as you asked."

Marnie's heart lifted again.

"I have watched you," Hoala said. "I watch all of them there. If you return to your people, I will find you again."

Marnie didn't try to argue. She didn't say, *They aren't my people.* From Hoala's perspective, all humans must seem the same. A single species, all with similar characteristics. Even a woman who could fly was still a human. Just as a penguin that swam rather than flew was still a bird.

"You'll teach me if I go back," Marnie said, wanting to make sure she understood Hoala's condition. "But not if I leave."

"I have to remain close," Hoala said.

Marnie nodded that she understood. Even though she wasn't sure that she did.

Hoala had some duty, maybe, or at least some preference to stay close to the Factory and watch what its inhabitants did.

Maybe the aliens who left their technology behind wanted to know what the earthlings intended to do with it.

But maybe Marnie could make her understand.

"I don't trust them," Marnie said. "They want to use me."

"They want you to teach them," Hoala said. "Just as you ask that I teach you."

Marnie stared at her for a moment. She breathed out a quiet, *Oh.* A chunk of ice seemed to chip off from Marnie's heart and fall away. She was so used to running, to bolting, to seeing everyone and everything as a threat.

But maybe that was just wrong. Maybe she was hurting herself as much as she suspected other people were so ready to hurt her. She had learned to trust Alice. Maybe there were a few other people she could trust, too.

Hoala gazed at Marnie in a tender and motherly way. She seemed to understand everything Marnie was thinking and feeling.

Another layer of ice around Marnie's heart melted away. Hoala smiled at her. Marnie got it.

"What do they want me to teach them?" Marnie asked. "I don't even know."

"How to fly," Hoala said. "Teach them to use their minds the way you do."

Marnie started to argue. She flew with her body, not with her mind. The pilots like Sharman Hix controlled their pods telepathically, but that wasn't how Marnie did it.

She just ran and pumped her arms and swam through the air. It was physical, not mental.

But then the truth of all of it hit her. Marnie nearly whispered another soft, *Oh.*

Of course it was mental. That was how her mother did it. She had brought Marnie's dreams of flying to life. The dreams weren't physical. They came from Marnie's mind.

"You really think I can teach them that?" Marnie asked.

"Do you believe I can teach you this?" Hoala asked, sweeping her webbed fingers upward from the transparent walls of the shelter to where they gathered together at their tip.

Marnie nodded. She did believe. Maybe she had no good reason for it, but she absolutely believed.

And because Hoala said she would teach her, that was all the confirmation Marnie needed. Hoala must believe it, too.

The pods were fanning out now in the distance. Marnie watched them fly. They wouldn't find her here, in Hoala's shelter. Marnie would have to go out and meet them.

She hated to leave. But she knew it was time. It was wrong of her to let the pilots go out searching again when she could see them. Wrong to let anyone worry anymore. She could picture Alice back at the Factory, genuinely concerned and waiting for word. Marnie couldn't do that to her any longer.

But even knowing she had to go, she still hesitated.

"When can I come back?" she asked.

"Whenever you wish," Hoala said. She gestured toward the pods. "But do not bring them with you."

Hoala swept her hand through the air. The transparent walls disappeared. Only the solid platform beneath their feet remained.

Marnie grabbed one more glance of Hoala's odd, silvery eyes before Hoala opened her wings wide and leapt into the wind.

Marnie opened her arms, too, and let herself fall. The snow-laden branches of the spruce tree flashed past her on the way down. Then Marnie caught a current and began swimming hard. Like someone tossed overboard, but determined to make it to shore.

Before long, one of the pilots must have seen her moving. A pod separated from the group and began speeding toward her. Soon the other four followed. Marnie continued stroking her arms through the air, but at an easier pace. She would get there when she did.

For now, she just wanted to enjoy flying. Enjoy the feeling of wind slipping along her skin. The cold winter morning stinging her face. The smell of the evergreen forest below.

Maybe she didn't have to run anymore. Maybe she could stay in one place, and still be free.

Marnie was willing to stick around for now and find out.

HIGHER

1

Sharman Hix was sweating. That rancid kind of flop sweat. She could smell it. Her glands and pores reacting to some mental or emotional signal and saying, *Better dump some of this out or you're gonna drown in toxic soup.*

Outside her pod the world was cold. Snowy white and cold. But inside, just Sharman alone with her machine, piloting the bubble-shaped wingless aircraft, she was working hard, perspiring, not panicking yet, but concerned.

Sharman had always thought of the pods as living, sentient beings rather than cold mechanical crafts. Like temperamental horses, she told the pilots she trained. You weren't just piloting a pod, you were developing a relationship with it. Treat it well. Talk to it with your mind. Let it get to know you while you learn how to fly it.

Talking to it mentally was the only way to control it. The pods had no visible means of powering or directing them. Just the lighted bands the pilots wore snug to their heads, over the skin-tight hoods of their special flight suits. The bands allowed the pilots to communicate telepathically with the pods. Weird and wonderful and still something new for Sharman to learn every day, even six years after she first started.

She was twenty-four and had being doing this since she was recruited at age eighteen. Her life took a turn then, one she eagerly embraced.

She came to the Factory, the concrete facility hidden deep under a mountain in the Wasatch range outside Salt Lake City, Utah. Came straight from the desert of Phoenix, Arizona. Had to adapt from minute one. It was February, ridiculously cold out, and Sharman wasn't dressed properly for the weather. She didn't have those kinds of clothes. Her new boss, Major Fritz Zimholt, had to lend her his own puffy down-filled coat while he took her on a tour of his facility.

He didn't bother showing her the living quarters or anything beneath the first floor. He started with the hangar. Smart man. That was the only thing Sharman cared about.

They stood together on the concrete floor inside the vast underground shelter. Sharman bundled Major Zimholt's coat around her. She was so much shorter than him, it almost reached all the way to her calves.

He didn't say much at first, just let her look. There were hundreds of pods sitting in the hangar, lined up in neat rows.

They were perfect spheres, half the size of a two-seater compact car. Their bottom halves were gray. The tops were all down, like convertibles. They sat there looking like the bottom halves of a plastic capsule, the kind you'd get out of a vending machine and that held a kid's cheap tiny toy.

Sharman liked the way the pods looked. So different from any kind of airplane. And not like any spaceship she'd seen in pictures or in movies or on TV.

"So that's what I'm gonna fly?"

Major Zimholt confirmed it. Sharman had planned on flying fighter jets before Major Zimholt recruited her. He claimed that the pods were more powerful than anything she would have flown for the Air Force. Looking at them, like giant beach balls, it was hard to believe it.

The two of them stood in the hangar and watched while a few of Major Zimholt's pilots loaded into their aircrafts. They wore funny one-piece suits that made them look like scuba divers. They pulled up their tight hoods and snugged them around their faces, then reached into the open pods and took out lighted headbands they settled around their heads.

"Head harness," Major Zimholt told her. "It allows them to control the pod."

The pilots climbed into their spheres. The see-through lids smoothly rose over them and settled against the lower gray bases. Then the first two pods at the front of their respective rows bubbled upward toward the ceiling, and popped out through matching holes.

Then two more pilots, two more pods, and off they went to fly. Like an assembly line, not a lot of fuss to it, just get in your craft and go.

Sharman Hix had come to the Factory not knowing what

her future would hold. Not for sure. She only had Major Zimholt's promises.

But seeing the pods, knowing she could start training to fly them that very afternoon, that she'd be flying tomorrow and every day, out there doing what she loved—Sharman's heart leapt over the bar. She was *in*. Sold. Ready to suit up and go the very next second.

Six years and over four thousand flights later, there was still so much Sharman didn't know about the pods. Starting with where they came from. Who invented them. How Major Zimholt ended up with them at his facility.

She understood why they were kept secret. That one was easy to get. For one thing, the pods weren't ready for ordinary use. The military wasn't going to let these loose on its pilots and watch them die in droves. It took a special touch—a special mind—to pilot a pod properly. Sharman had it. A lot of pilots didn't. She had seen plenty of them crash and die over the last several years.

Then there was the matter of national security. Other nations might have similar craft, but somehow Sharman doubted it. The way Major Zimholt talked about their responsibility to keep this a secret, Sharman assumed there weren't other facilities like the Factory hiding out there under any other mountains around the world. Maybe on islands. Maybe in other secret places she knew nothing about. But she just had the feeling, deep in her gut, that these were the only pods on Earth. She continued to operate under that assumption. She trained her pilots to do the same.

Sharman was at the top of her game. There was no one

better at flying the pods. No brag, just fact. She was the best at what she did.

Until today.

"Focus," she heard Marnie Stemple say through their linked head harnesses. Marnie's voice sounded as clear as if she were scrunched up next to Sharman inside the pod.

"I am focused," Sharman snapped. But she knew Marnie was right. Sharman might be the best pilot here, but right now she was failing.

The pod just stopped responding to Sharman at all. She asked it to go up, it went sideways. She told it to slow down, it doubled its speed.

Like a bratty, willful child. Like a horse bolting and charging away. Sharman kept trying to soothe it, to master it, but the damn thing had a dangerous mind of its own.

And right now, even though Sharman had asked it nicely to climb, the pod was diving down the length of a mountain, heading for the hard and deadly ground.

Sharman swiped sweat out of her right eye. *Concentrate—*

"Concentrate," Marnie said.

Sharman growled and gave it up.

"Help," she said, and Marnie did. Immediately. She stood on the top of a snow-covered cliff above where Sharman was practicing, and from there she had no trouble taking command. Her own head harness let her communicate tele-pathically with the pod.

Training wheels, Sharman had called it, when she was the one on land and Marnie was out here in the hefty wind piloting Sharman's pod for the very first time.

Sharman couldn't help remembering how smug she felt

that day. Like she knew more than some woman who could fly through the air on her own. No pod required for Marnie Stemple. Just a few beats of her scrawny arms.

Marnie brought the pod back up to the cliff face and lightly set it down. Sharman sat in her seat for half a minute more, just catching her breath. And swallowing her pride.

Then she popped the lid—at least the pod allowed her to do that—and she reached down and put her boots on before climbing out onto the snow.

The other pilots wore the soft leather boots whenever they flew. It was part of the full flight suit. It had been designed as part of the package.

But Sharman always flew barefoot. She thought it gave her a better edge. She pressed her bare skin against what she thought of as the skin inside the pod, and let it feel a greater connection with her, flesh on flesh.

But Sharman climbed out of her pod feeling like right now she didn't know it at all. Like it was just a cold metal machine and she was just some hired worker here to run it.

Marnie stood wrapped in a long black down-filled coat. She handed Sharman her gray one. Sharman quickly put it on. The morning was freezing. It was mid-January, so of course it was cold. Sharman still had desert blood in her veins. She had never adapted to the mountain winters.

"Okay," she said to Marnie, "tell me everything I did wrong."

Marnie gave her a sympathetic look. She wasn't trying to be cruel. But her words cut Sharman to the bone.

"You didn't do any of it right," Marnie said. "It's like you didn't hear anything I said. We … we might as well start over." She shrugged. Sharman could see she was uncomfortable. Like she wasn't used to giving criticism. Or maybe she thought Sharman hadn't already spent her life learning how to take it. "The way you were flying before I got here was probably good enough," Marnie said. "It's just … if you want to do it better."

Sharman groaned. She felt like grabbing a handful of snow and hurling it at Marnie. But not really. It wasn't the woman's fault.

If Marnie was right, she was right. And based on Sharman's miserable performance just now, she had to admit the woman was right.

"Let me just pout for a minute," Sharman said. She wasn't be sarcastic, she meant it. She sat cross-legged a few feet back from the edge of the cliff and let her thick puffy coat insulate her from the snow.

She had brought a thermos full of coffee this morning, more for the warmth than the caffeine. She unscrewed the top and poured out a cup. She didn't bother offering any to Marnie, who always said no.

Five days. Five days so far. And still no real progress. In fact, Sharman's performance was getting worse. It was like the pod knew it was being managed, and it didn't like it one bit. Sharman could have switched to one of the other ones, maybe given herself a fresh start, but a stubborn streak made her stick to the same pod day after day, determined to connect with it in a whole new way.

The way Marnie was trying to teach her.

"Tell me again," Sharman said. She cradled the cup of

coffee between her cold fingers. "Tell me like it's a bedtime story. I'm going to close my eyes and listen."

And Sharman did. She sat like a kid during story time and listened to everything Marnie said.

Marnie described for Sharman again what it was like to fly just with the power of her body. How she moved. What she thought about. What she felt.

It was the next step in Sharman's evolution as a pilot. Sharman knew it. She could taste it, so close to the tip of her tongue. Feel it and think it, right on the edge of her hungry mind. No one was making her do this, it was her own idea. As soon as she saw Marnie flying, Sharman knew she had so much more to learn.

And Marnie challenged Sharman's thinking right away, the first time they talked about it.

"Stop thinking of the pods as separate," Marnie said. "They don't have to be. What if you started feeling them as part of your own body?"

Sharman's mind churned. She could see the sense in it. A new ideal she had never thought possible.

The pods were living creatures in their way, that much was still true.

But maybe Sharman wasn't riding them like horses. Maybe she could be one with the horse instead. Melded somehow into its limbs and muscles and organs. Running along *inside* it, feeling its heart pump and its legs eat up the ground.

Or like a bird, the way Marnie tried to explain it. Not riding on its back between its wings. Sitting inside it and flapping those wings herself.

It was all so new, so impossible sounding, and yet so tantalizingly close to being real, it made Sharman's head feel like it would spin right off of her neck.

The lure of it was so exciting, she knew she needed to try.

Even if so far the results were nothing but ugly.

Sharman tossed out what was left of the coffee in her cup. It melted a dark hole in the snow.

She stood and shucked off her coat. Marnie let hers drop, too. She had been standing around too long. Every hour or so, Marnie needed to fly.

Sharman climbed back into her craft. She pulled her boots off and settled the harness on her head. Marnie took her matching harness off. She didn't like to fly with it. She set it on top of her coat, near the thermos.

"So don't do anything crazy for a while," Marnie warned her. "I won't be able to save you."

Sharman wasn't used to being a beginner. She hated it more than she was willing to show. She asked the pod nicely to please put the dome up over her head.

Marnie ran and jumped from the ledge. Sharman watched with envy how easy it was for Marnie to fly.

I want to be her when I grow up.

Sharman chuckled to herself, a little embarrassed that she put her longing into words. She hadn't meant to think it, but there it was.

She wondered what the pod might be thinking in return. She hoped it wasn't insulted, as if Sharman didn't want it.

"Oh, but I love flying in the pod even more," Sharman said out loud. She hoped she sounded convincing.

And she should. She did love it. It was just that she wanted to feel different while she did it. She wanted to feel like she *was* the pod, not just its pilot. Like she was this little spaceship zipping through the air. That's what she hoped Marnie could teach her.

Sharman took a deep breath. Cleared her mind. Exactly the way she trained the other pilots to do.

Then she turned to a fresh page. She needed to get back to flying well.

"Where would you like to go?" Sharman asked her pod. Maybe that would make a difference. Connect them again. Bring them back closer.

The pod responded at once.

It rose into the air and zipped off to the right. And it kept accelerating, faster than Sharman expected it to go. But she wasn't worried. She had been in pods plenty of times when they reached what she thought was probably their maximum speed. It took nerve and Sharman had it. She wasn't going to back down now.

She settled back into her pilot's seat. She pressed her arms into the armrest and spread her bare toes against the angled platform along the floor. She purposely made her shoulders drop. She let her head lean back against its support. Like this was just a casual cruise somewhere, like it was no big deal, just a girl and her pod out enjoying a crisp clear morning. Seeing what they could see.

The pod increased its speed. It continued bowling through the air, racing south away from the Factory.

It seemed to know exactly where it was going.

And Sharman had no idea where that was.

2

It was just past nine in the morning, but the sun was still barely showing its face. That was the problem with winter, besides the obvious cold. The days started too late and ended too early. Sharman barely had time to get going before it seemed like sunset was here again.

Down in the valley, in Salt Lake City, sunrise was sometime after seven. But the mountains around the Factory were so high, it took another few hours for daylight to really take hold up here.

Sharman had gotten used to never seeing the sunrise for herself anymore. At least not in person. Her bedroom was down on the second floor. There were no windows there or anywhere else. What would they show anyway? Just solid rock. The entire facility was burrowed under the mountain.

But there were cameras up topside that broadcast a live feed round the clock so that everyone could always see the weather. Sharman hung a TV screen up on the east wall of her small, functional room, in between some of her posters. She defaulted to streaming in from the east feed so that the sun always rose there in the mornings, just like she used to see it out her bedroom window growing up.

She could scroll through the other camera feeds any time she needed to, but she was hardly ever in her bedroom except to sleep. She'd rather go see the weather for herself. She was here to fly, not to hang out indoors. Any hour she wasn't piloting one of the pods, learning how to do it better, teaching other pilots how to do it better—that was a waste of sixty minutes. She had to eat and sleep and keep herself in fit flying form—*right and tight,* one of her old flight instructors used to call it—but other than that, Sharman wasn't interested in just sitting around and thinking or talking about flying. She'd rather go do it. All the time.

So waiting until sunrise to get started every day—come *on.* January mornings killed her. At least it was after winter solstice, which meant that each day was getting longer and brighter, even if it was just by a few minutes. She'd take it. Better than in December, when each day got shorter and darker.

Back in Phoenix where Sharman spent the first eighteen years of her life, the sun rose early and felt like it hardly set. Even now, her internal clock still got her up at five o'clock every morning, summer, winter, it didn't matter. She sprang out of bed. Things to do. Life was already too short. Get to it.

Seven hours of sleep, exactly. In bed by nine-thirty every night, read for half an hour, lights out by ten. She tried to get the other pilots on the same schedule, but most of them were young and thought they knew better.

The pods needed fresh minds. Every single day. Show up yawning, distracted, *hung over,* for godsake, and you weren't going to last in the pilot program. Sharman Hix was the leader, and she would see to that.

Pilots died. Easily. Sharman had seen more of that than she ever wanted to see. Every time she kicked someone out of the program, whether they appreciated it or not, Sharman knew she had just saved their life. Let them go fly fighter jets or rockets. Safer than the pods unless you knew what you were doing.

Sharman had a coffee maker in her room, set to automatically brew at four fifty-eight AM. She sat in bed with her first cup and made notes about what she intended to accomplish for the day. Coffee done, change into workout clothes. At that time of morning, five twenty-five, she usually had the second-floor gym all to herself.

She did the same routine every day. Keeping things the same allowed her mind to roam. She got her best ideas while she ran on the treadmill for the first thirty minutes. She dictated notes to herself on her watch recorder. She would add them to her list later.

The second thirty minutes she lifted weights, alternating upper and lower body on successive days. Today was mostly arms. Then back to her room for a shower. Then breakfast in the second-floor cafeteria, provided by the excellent cooks on staff. Another alternating schedule: oatmeal and fruit one day, eggs and whole wheat toast the next. And always a second cup of coffee. Gotta get the machine up and running.

That was how she thought of herself: a machine. It was up to her to keep everything going in prime condition. Sharman wasn't just waiting for her future. Things didn't just happen, they didn't just come. Sharman went out and got them.

Looking at her life, some people probably thought she got a lucky break back when she was eleven. But Sharman sought it out. She worked for it. She made it hers.

She was a small, skinny black girl—still was, not much had changed. She was still only five-foot-two, rounding up, and from far away probably didn't look much bigger than when she was in fifth grade.

Back then she was all legs, had long bony arms, and her mother kept Sharman's short curly black hair trimmed close to her scalp. Sharman wore plain clothes, usually the same kind of thing as her brother. Shorts and a T-shirt in summer, shorts and a sweatshirt in winter. Simple.

She wasn't here to make a statement with her hair or her clothes or anything else. She didn't need anyone to notice her. That wasn't what she was about. Let them pass over her, as long as they left her alone to do her own thing: read as much as she wanted, play as much as she wanted.

Sharman had been wicked smart as a little girl, and she was happy if only her parents and her teachers knew it. She wasn't trying to impress the other kids. On the playground she was just about running and climbing and doing flips off the bar and pumping her legs on the swing so she could launch herself from up high. Sharman Hix was born wanting to be airborne.

One of the advantages of living where they did, in one of the more crowded and low-income sections of Phoenix, was that sometimes there were charitable programs through Sharman's school. Opportunities that weren't there for the richer kids in the richer districts.

At the beginning of the fifth grade school year, Sharman's teacher sent home a three-page printout, stapled at the left corner—Sharman could still picture every single detail about it—that listed the various extra-curricular programs available to the students that year. Chess club, orchestra, dance, gymnastics, arts and crafts, computer lab— and flight.

Flight.

It was the first time it was ever offered. Some retired Air Force officer had decided to start a pilot program for kids. The description said it was to help them focus, help them learn to love science and math, maybe get them interested in joining the Air Force themselves when they were older—and Sharman's eyes skipped over all of it, because she didn't care why it was supposed to be good for her, she just *wanted* it. Had to have it. Immediately.

She ran to school early the next morning and waited impatiently for the guidance counselor to get there.

"Sign me up for that one!" she told the counselor, pointing at the last item on the third page of the stapled handout. The counselor knew as well as Sharman's parents and teachers what a good student she was. Top grades, never a disciplinary problem—if it was based on merit, Sharman

Hix should be top of the list, whether she ran to school early that morning or not.

But joining the flight club wasn't based on merit. It didn't depend on good grades or intelligence or excellence of any kind. It was open to all kids, even the worst ones. Sharman couldn't believe it. But the counselor was serious.

The founder of the program, Lieutenant Colonel James Jackson, wanted to offer this opportunity to any kid who was interested. But he only had twelve spots. There was just one plane and only one other instructor besides him. Maybe if the program grew over time they'd have room for more kids, but for now he had to keep it small.

"But mine is the first name on the list," Sharman said. "Right?"

"First name," the counselor agreed. She typed it into her computer right in front of Sharman. But then the counselor turned back to face her, and let out a little sigh. Sharman knew that couldn't be good.

"If more than twelve kids sign up," the counselor said, "they'll probably have to pick names out of a hat. There's no guarantee. I'm sorry. That's how Mr. Jackson wants it. Fair to all kids."

But it wasn't fair at all. Sharman knew it and the counselor knew it. This was the only thing Sharman had ever asked for in her whole time at that school. She always went along. She was a quiet and dutiful girl. She did her work and then read her books until it was time to go out and play.

Sharman left the counselor's office in a numb kind of fog. She listened to the kids around her all day, and the next few days after that, trying to hear whether anyone else was going to sign up for flight.

A lot of them. Boys and girls both. Smart and not, both. Deserving and undeserving both.

Sharman could barely eat or sleep. Finally her mother asked her what was wrong.

Sharman had wanted to surprise her family when she got into the program, but she couldn't hold it in any longer. She poured out her heart. Every hope and dream. To be a *pilot*. To fly. "Mama, can you believe it?"

But Sharman's mother didn't just wait for things to come to her, either. She pulled out a notepad and set it in front of Sharman and told her, "You'd better write to that man yourself."

WHY I WANT TO FLY.

A two-page, heartfelt letter handwritten by an eleven-year-old girl to some gruff old Air Force Lieutenant Colonel she had never met, but who she hoped would be the answer to the biggest dream of her life.

By the time the lists of extracurricular clubs were posted on the board, Sharman knew from the counselor that thirty-seven kids had put in their names to learn to fly.

Sharman knew all of them. A few of them were serious, but not all. Some of them put their names down for every-thing, even chess club, even though they would probably hate it. It was more fun to stay after school and do stuff than to go home and play video games or just sit around.

Sharman pushed her way in between some of the bigger kids and breathlessly scanned the flight club list.

There she was, fourth alphabetically.

Sharman nearly shouted with joy. It was the start of a dream come true.

For the next seven years she devoted herself to being the best. She worked harder than anyone else, day after day. She was the top pilot in the program.

She decided to go higher, and not just be a pilot. Lieutenant Colonel Jackson thought she might be an astronaut some day. Sharman thought so, too.

She graduated from high school a semester early, in December. She was anxious to get going to college. One of the fancy east coast universities was giving her a full ride.

Sharman had her plan. Chemical engineering, physics, Air Force, NASA. Sharman knew her path.

Then on the morning of December twenty-first, she got a call from someone named Major Fritz Zimholt. He had a better plan. A way for Sharman to reach the stars on a shorter and more direct path.

Why should she waste her time on four long years of college, when he had instructors at his facility who would teach her everything she needed to know? If she wanted to fly—and one day wanted to pilot a ship into space—then Major Zimholt's people could offer her exactly the training and education she needed. All for free.

In exchange, Sharman had to agree to leave her old life behind, and commit to being one of Major Zimholt's test pilots. With all of the dangers that entailed.

Leaving her old life behind had been the hardest part.

But flying dangerous, temperamental aircraft? Let her at it.

First the pods, and then … something more. Major

Zimholt had hinted several times at there being an even larger craft someplace off property, just waiting for a pilot who had what it took to actually fly it.

Not just an aircraft, a *space*craft. Something that could take Sharman out to the stars.

She tried to find out more, but Major Zimholt never told her as much about it as she wanted. But Sharman understood. She could be that pilot if she kept on working harder than anyone every day, and pushed herself upward to a whole other level.

That was why she needed Marnie to teach her. Because Sharman wasn't going high enough on her own.

She even had that as a motivational sign in her bedroom. Along with a dozen different posters of star systems and various planets.

HIGHER, the sign said. Not only Earth, it reminded her, but more. Not only airplanes, not only pods, but her own spaceship some day to command.

Right now, though, Sharman's future as a pilot wasn't as lofty as she liked to see it. She had given up control of her pod and it was still racing away with her to the south.

There were high peaks and jagged rocky ridges to her left and right. The Wasatch range was about two hundred and fifty miles long, north to south, but only eighteen miles across. There were mountains wherever she looked. Snow-covered, solid rock mountains.

Sharman kept telling herself to relax. The pods weren't suicidal. If they crashed it was because pilots had done something wrong.

"Where are you?" Marnie asked her over the head

harness. She must have finished flying and come back to the cliff to resume their lesson.

"Way off to the right," Sharman said, trying to keep her voice steady. She didn't want the pod to know how unsettled she was.

"Well, come back," Marnie said. "Where I can see you."

"Um … hold on." Sharman rolled her shoulders and shook out her hands. She had to dump off some of her stress.

She pictured the pod slowing down. Returning to a nice little cruise. Then turning about and sailing at a reasonable speed back to where Marnie could watch them from the cliff.

But even though Sharman could see the images clearly in her mind, her pod ignored her and continued speeding south.

"Hey, do me a favor," Sharman said to Marnie. She cleared her throat and tried to keep it all calm. "Stick that harness down the front of your flight suit so you have it with you. And then see if you can catch up with me. We're going pretty fast."

Sharman understood why Marnie didn't like to fly with it on. She was always afraid the wind might whip it off of her hood. It wasn't the kind of thing you wanted to lose.

Silence for a moment inside Sharman's pod. Then Marnie's voice right beside her, sounding concerned. "What's going on?"

"I asked it where it wanted to go, and it's showing me."

Silence again. Then, "Oh."

"So … maybe you could—"

"Signing off right now," Marnie said. "I'm coming as fast as I can."

Sharman's heart raced right along with the pod. She had seen pilots pass out when their minds got overwhelmed and their heart rates skyrocketed. It was why Sharman kept a head harness of her own, linked to the pods of the pilots she was training. She had saved more than a few of them from ending up on some joyride like the one her pod was taking her on now.

Mistake. Huge mistake. Why had she given the pod its head? Like loosening the reins and telling a galloping horse to have at it. Go wherever you want. Don't mind me, I'm just along for the ride.

There was no way Marnie Stemple could catch them. She wasn't even a fraction this fast, and the pod already had a huge lead.

"Ready to turn around now?" Sharman asked in a friendly way.

But the pod continued its sprint toward some destination of its own.

3

tart over. Lesson one.

Sharman raised her arms and then set them carefully back down on the arm rests. Normally the pod's seat adjusted to the pilot and molded around him or her, but this pod had already done that.

Sharman scooched back into her seat again to have as much of her body in contact with it. She lifted her bare feet and then set them down again on the platform. As if by doing any of this she was resetting the control. Shutting the computer off and turning it back on.

But there was no computer. The pod could think for itself. How many times had Sharman tried to explain that to the pilots that she trained? *We're the pods' partners, not their masters.*

Right now the pod was doing whatever it wanted. Just like Sharman invited it to do.

Marnie's voice came back inside the pod. Her breath

sounded labored, like she had been flying her lungs out. She must have landed somewhere briefly so she could pull out the harness and stick it on her head to check in.

"Where are you now?" Marnie panted.

"You can't see me yet?" Sharman asked. She wasn't surprised. She knew they had come too far.

It was part of her personal training, learning to estimate time and distance. She checked herself throughout the day, guessing exactly what time it was, then checking her watch to see if she was right.

There were no displays inside the pod to tell her altitude or speed, but the Factory tracked it with various measuring devices of its own. Sharman checked her records every night, and the records of all the pilots she trained that day, to see if her estimates of distance, altitude, and speed were close to being right.

It was a learnable skill, and she was getting better at it all the time. She played the game now, starting with a guess at the time. Maybe around nine forty-five. She checked her watch. Close. It was nine thirty-six.

Sharman guessed at the pod's exact speed and altitude. She wouldn't know if she was right until she saw the records tonight.

But tonight seemed a long time away, even with the short January daylight.

If the pod continued traveling at this speed, Sharman might find herself over Arizona before dark. And then what? On to Mexico? Somewhere further south? Where was this pod trying to go? And why? As far as Sharman knew, it had never been this far from the Factory home base.

Marnie again, still breathless from exertion. "I'm going to keep going. Are you still traveling south?"

"Yes." Sharman described the landscape around her. The particular mountains, the shape of the stream below her right now, like a dark gray line threading through the otherwise blank canvas of white snow.

Sharman resisted saying *Hurry*. Saying *Help*. It wasn't just Marnie listening, it was the pod, too.

Sharman tried again to speak to the craft. "It's beautiful out here." She could hear the stress in her voice. She shook out her hands again. She rolled her shoulders. "But hey, let's go back now. I've gotta pee. Let's go see what Marnie is doing."

Like begging a toddler who was throwing a fit. *Don't you want to see Santa? Would you like some candy? How about a toy?*

But Sharman thought she could feel a difference. Maybe the pod slowed down, just a little.

So she kept talking. Saying nonsense. Just filling the air. Like someone in one of those cop shows who was told to keep the bad guy on the phone until they could trace the call.

She was stalling for time, hoping Marnie would find her at some point. Hoping Marnie could intervene and bring this pod back in line. But even at its slightly reduced speed, it was still much faster than Sharman had ever seen Marnie fly.

Sharman wondered if Major Zimholt was seeing this. If someone had alerted him yet that something had gone wrong.

Maybe he would send out other pilots from Sharman's team, like life guards jumping into the swells of the sea.

She was sure to be demoted. She had taken a risk and it had blown up her face. She wanted to be better than anyone and worthy of the bigger ship Major Zimholt had in mind, but obviously someone else would now rise past her to take Sharman's place.

There was pain now on the left of her chest. Sharman pressed her hand there. She could feel her bounding heart.

There was pain in her arms. Like electric current. Then she felt it in her thighs and down to her feet.

Some kind of stress response. It had to be. Sharman was young and healthy, a specimen, a machine.

But maybe the pod's speed was doing a number on her nervous system. She had never tested it at speeds this high.

Then Sharman pitched forward in her seat. The pod had come to an abrupt and complete halt. It hovered motionless above one of the peaks.

Sharman breathed shallowly, quietly, while her heart hammered loudly in her ears. She didn't know what to do. So she just waited and watched.

The pod jerked forward about a foot. Then back the same distance. Like it wasn't sure. Just like Sharman.

And then it started rising, slowly and smoothly. The way the pods bubbled to the ceiling inside the hangar.

This was better. Slow was better. Sharman readjusted herself in the seat. She went through the same motions as before, resetting her arms, spine, feet.

"Ready to go back now?" she asked in a calm, friendly

voice. Even though she wanted to shout out a command to just *DO IT.*

The pod continued rising. Then it picked up speed again. Then more. It was back to its breakneck pace.

"Hey, Marnie," Sharman called. On the off chance she might hear it coming through her suit. But Marnie didn't answer. The harness needed to be on her head.

Marnie would be flying south as fast as she could.

But she wasn't flying up. She didn't know where to look for Sharman now.

Sharman gazed all around her, trying to memorize some landmarks. In case Marnie got in contact before it was too late.

But the winter sky was crowded with clouds. And the pod rose even with them, then up inside to where it was folded within the white. It didn't stay there, but kept on traveling upward until Sharman could look down and see the clouds below them.

She had no chance of seeing Marnie anymore. Or of Marnie seeing her.

Sharman couldn't panic. That wasn't going to help anything at all. She was along for the ride. At least the pod wasn't heading into a mountain and trying to kill her.

Sharman guessed at the time. Maybe ten twenty-two. She checked her watch. Close. It was ten sixteen.

She guessed at the altitude. Part of her training at the Factory involved meteorology. She should be able to estimate altitude based on the type and position of the clouds. They might be around ten thousand feet up now. But that was just a guess. The craft continued climbing.

As soon as Sharman saw a passenger plane, she knew they must be up to at least thirty thousand feet.

The plane's pilot wouldn't be able to see her. The pods were only visible to the pilots of other pods. And to Marnie, whose flight suit was made of the same material that covered their exterior.

But Sharman's pod saw or sensed or at least reacted to the passenger plane, and it steered well clear of it and remained out of its path.

Sharman felt like a fisherman sitting in his tiny boat, trying to dodge the ocean liner dominating the sea.

"Where are you?" Marnie again, thank God. Probably miles away, but still sounding like she was close enough to be sitting in Sharman's lap.

"Straight up." Sharman described the last patch of scenery she saw before they entered the clouds. "I gotta tell you, this has got me pretty spooked."

The pod jerked to a halt. Sharman held her breath. Maybe it would take pity on her, knowing she was scared.

Maybe that was her mistake, pretending everything was fine. Putting false cheerfulness into her voice, making the pod think Sharman was enjoying this crazy excursion.

"I'm scared," she said again, speaking mostly to the pod. But Marnie heard it, too, and said, "Hold on, I'm trying to find you."

The pod started up again. But not so fast anymore. Still it kept climbing. Higher and higher.

The sky was blue up here, a much darker blue than below. Sharman knew the strata, the different layers of altitude. As you rose higher away from the earth, the color went from royal blue to purplish blue and eventually you passed fully into black. And then … space, at some point. But not without an immense amount of thrust to get you past the first sixty-two miles above the earth.

This little pod didn't have enough power. It couldn't possibly get that far. So where did it think it was going?

The pod halted again. It hovered and waited.

And then Sharman looked up through the clear dome of her pod.

There was a ship there. Silent and immense, like an enormous whale gliding through the sea. It passed above the pod, maybe a hundred yards away. Maybe further. A lot further. Sharman was having trouble adjusting her sight to the size.

The pod shuddered like a boat getting bounced by a passing wave. Like a small craft feeling the wake of a larger vessel.

Sharman stared at the belly of the ship as it passed overhead. It was dark gray, like the lower half of her pod.

It was flat on the bottom. Long and rectangular, rather than round. Size? Maybe ten football fields. No, probably much more.

Her eyes couldn't take it all in. It was too close to see it from end to end. The ship kept passing above her and went on and on. Like trying to wait for the end of a train and finally here it was. But until the last car, you couldn't guess how much longer it was just from watching it speed by.

"Is this … do you know this ship?" Sharman asked her pod. She didn't know what to expect. It had never answered her before.

And it didn't answer her now. It just stayed holding in place. The ship glided onward. And it still wasn't done.

But it wasn't possible. Sharman knew that. Vessels that large weren't traveling in Earth's atmosphere.

That thing was the size of a spaceship. Which meant it belonged much higher than where Sharman was now.

She wasn't wrong about where she was. She wasn't wrong about still being close to Earth. She might be higher than she had ever gone in either a pod or a plane, but she hadn't slipped past the planet's gravity. She wasn't in space.

But she was too high for Marnie to come. It would be hard for her to breathe. And no matter how remarkable Marnie Stemple was, she still had a human body and it had its limits.

Sharman was the only person who was going to see this.

The only witness to something that couldn't be true, but she was watching it with her sharp, keen eyes. *Here there be dragons,* the ancient mapmakers wrote on their maps. Faithful to the reports from courageous mariners who survived the monsters they saw out at sea.

Sharman thought of the posters back in her room. Where should she draw this ship? It didn't belong where she saw it, so where should it go? Above the Earth, but not too far above. Below the stars, but how far below?

And why was she given this gift—why her? Was it a vision? How could it be real?

Sharman continued staring up through the dome of her pod, watching the ship make its slow, majestic way. She estimated that twenty minutes passed before she saw the end of it finally come into view. She checked her watch. She was off by four minutes.

The rear of the ship had a snub, blunt edge. Like the end of a kitchen counter when you looked at it from the side.

Sharman tried to guess how tall the ship was. Ten stories? Higher? She didn't know. She tried to burn the image inside her mind so she could draw it later and try to measure from that.

Then the ship was gone. The sky was empty again. Back to dark blue, or maybe closer to purple.

Sharman had forgotten about the pod. She felt like she had been sitting in some theater. Or a planetarium, just watching the show.

But the pod began moving again. The show was over for it, too. It started a slow and reasonable descent.

Air rushed up Sharman's throat. As though the atmosphere was passing through her.

Sharman swallowed hard. Her throat felt dry and hot. Her cheeks were hot, too, like she might have a fever.

Her heart felt raw and swollen. It hurt as it beat in her chest. Sharman felt small. Just a small pinpoint out in the vast sky.

The pod was warm all around her. Keeping her safe and warm. Cradling her. Taking her down.

Sharman blinked. Cleared her eyes. Swallowed hard again. She felt like crying, but she didn't know why. There was a feeling inside her too big to try to explain.

She leaned forward from her seat and reached out to the transparent dome in front of her. She patted it, like she was patting a good dog.

Like she was patting the sweating neck of a horse who had taken her safely through battle. *Good boy. Hell of a boy. You saved us.*

Sharman settled her arms onto the arms of her chair. She leaned back and closed her eyes. Her bare feet spread onto the platform below. Sharman breathed easily and melted into the chair.

This was what it felt like. This was what Marnie meant. But she was wrong about how Sharman could find it.

Not by trying. Not by willing it. Not by trying to be strategic or tricky. Not by listening to Marnie tell her again how it felt to fly.

It was by letting go. Letting the pod tell her what it wanted. Letting the pod give Sharman what she wanted most of all.

The pod had gone higher. Just like Sharman wanted to go. But like Sharman never would have believed they could do.

What was that ship? Was it real? It had to be. Sharman knew it. But she couldn't explain how something that big could be sailing through that piece of sky.

But the pod knew it was there. It knew it was real, too. It knew when the ship would pass by, and it had raced to bring Sharman there in time.

Sharman lifted her arms and hugged them around the arms of her seat. She leaned forward and kissed the nearest part of the pod.

She watched the clouds reappear, first at her feet, then at her head, and then they were through them, and she saw a speck far off in the distance.

Just another tiny human. Too small to be important. A little pinpoint of gray out in the soft blue sky.

Marnie saw Sharman, too. She started heading her way. But she came slowly. She had to be exhausted.

"Let's find a place to land," Sharman told the pod. "Marnie needs to rest. Maybe you do, too."

The pod closed the distance to Marnie, then found a flat spot where they both could land. It set itself down on a blanket of snow.

Marnie was still in the air a short distance away. Sharman sat where she was. She was in no hurry. She was perfectly at home.

Her body felt different. Her mind felt bigger. Her heart … how could she explain it? It was like it had blown outward from her chest somewhere up there in the dark blue. She could feel something touching it. Something warm and alive. Something not human, but still wanting to be connected. The pod had met Sharman's raw heart out there where they watched the ship. Then Sharman's heart folded the pod inside it and resumed its regular beating.

One. They were one. So this was how it felt.

Sharman felt the pod surrounding her in warmth. She extended her own warmth right back to it. *You're safe. We're together.*

Marnie had been right. Once Sharman got it, the connection felt effortless. It was both as simple and as mysterious as the way the pods adjusted their interiors to allow the pilots to comfortably breathe. Weaving herself into the pod felt just as natural as that.

Sharman watched as Marnie landed wearily onto the

snow. Marnie's knees sagged forward and she reached out her hands to catch herself before she collapsed completely. Her head hung for a moment, but then she lifted her chin and twisted to look inside the pod. She met Sharman's gaze and returned her smile.

Marnie reached inside her flight suit and pulled out her lighted harness. She positioned it over her hood.

"Are you all right?" Marnie asked as soon as she knew Sharman could hear her.

"Yes. Are you?"

Marnie crossed her arms over her chest and grabbed her biceps in opposite hands. She groaned, but she didn't seem unhappy. Still, the flight must have worn her down to the bone.

Times like these, Sharman wished the pods could carry two. But they were perfectly proportioned only for one.

The air around Sharman felt cooler. The sound of her breathing was fainter. Like going from a small enclosed room into the hallway. Everything felt and sounded different because the space was larger.

Sharman looked behind her. Normally she saw the rounded lid of the sphere just as she saw it in front of her, the same size and distance away.

But just as the pods molded their seats to the different bodies of the various pilots, Sharman's pod adjusted its entire size and shape to suit her current needs.

The lid of the pod rose above Sharman's head. It traveled backward along its new oblong length.

There was space behind Sharman's seat for one passenger to rest comfortably on the floor.

Marnie and Sharman locked eyes. And then Marnie stumbled onto her weary legs and climbed on board.

The lid closed again. The remade pod rose from the snow.

Good boy. Hell of a boy. Thank you.

Sharman wondered if Major Zimholt had any idea how much more these pods could do. Once again she let her pod have its head. She knew it would take them home.

"Where were you?" Marnie asked. She sounded so tired. Sharman expected her to pass out asleep any minute.

"It wanted to show me a ship," Sharman said.

"What ship?"

"I have no idea," Sharman said. "But I saw it."

She tried to picture it again, with every detail she remembered. She would have to draw it as soon as she got back. Even before she told Major Zimholt about it.

And how was she going to explain how she felt now about the pod? She needed to keep it sounding technical. Otherwise it was going to sound like love.

Sharman could hear Marnie's breathing behind her seat. Soft, rhythmic, sleeping.

What ship? Marnie had asked her. A logical question. But Sharman could only guess at the answer.

Her pod knew her heart's desire. To go higher. Sharman just didn't know it was possible to do. Not now, not yet, as she was.

She wanted to command a ship some day. Maybe the one the pod showed her was meant to be hers. Or maybe it was just supposed to be a thrill: *Look at this! Can you believe it?*

Or maybe it had nothing at all to do with her. Maybe it

was the pod longing to see a ship that it knew. Maybe it came from that ship. Maybe all of the pods did. Sharman didn't have a clue.

She needed time to process everything that happened. She needed to know what it all meant. She didn't feel ready at all to explain it.

Sharman relaxed back into her seat. She pressed her fingers into the indentations at the end of her chair arms. She spread her toes against the platform beneath her feet. She could feel the pod's heartbeat fluttering against her bare skin. Fluttering *through* her.

She could feel the connection reaching into her nerves and her muscles and her heart. Branching everywhere inside her, like roots spreading underground from a tree.

The pod adjusted its heartbeat to match Sharman's own. And Sharman shifted her mind.

She understood what Marnie had been trying to teach her. She understood the connection. Sharman didn't need to ask the pod to do anything or tell it or direct it any way. She wasn't separate anymore, sitting inside and trying to fly it. For now and for as long as she wanted to be, she *was* it.

Sharman relaxed. She closed her eyes for a moment to set her course, her speed, and her altitude.

Then with as little effort as it took to raise her foot from the platform beneath it, Sharman lifted off of the snow and rose into the air and carried herself and Marnie back home.

SEEKER

1

People were all the same. This year, thirty years ago, five hundred years ago. Probably even cavemen. Killers, not killers. Dishonest, honest. Good people, bad people. The human condition. It all came down to character. Probably something you were born with, like people who could curl their tongue or couldn't.

Alice Kern stared at the computer screen. Names. Dates.

Familiar.

Family.

She was down on the second floor of the Factory in one of the computer rooms. Down, because the floors here were underground. There were three floors total, all of them spanning the same length and width as the decoy private regional airport sitting above them on one of the steep, rugged mountains of the Wasatch Mountain Range near Salt Lake City, Utah.

Whoever had built the Factory initially must have had

millions to throw at the project. The construction of the bunker inside the mountain was a feat of design and engineering. Alice guessed it would have taken years to blast and dig and carve their way this far underground, then build all the molds and supports, install plumbing and electricity to hundreds of individual rooms, add the special features needed in the first floor hangar to allow the experimental aircraft within it to operate and to secretly come and go, and then at some point they had poured in enough concrete to create the actual structure. Impressive.

Whoever did the finish work had taken pride in their work. The walls were perfectly smooth and seamless, like the bowl of a swimming pool. The Factory could have felt cold and institutional, but instead it felt strangely cozy. Like an animal's underground burrow. It could have felt closed in and smelly, like an old gym, but the air was kept fresh through some means, and Alice never detected the slightest rude odor of someone else's cooking or their heavy cologne or perfume or their sweat from working out.

Her room here was nothing like her studio apartment back in San Diego. In some ways it was nicer. Smaller, but newer feeling, even though she knew it had been built decades ago. The furniture was simple and modern. Not much of it. Just a queen-sized bed with a navy blue bedspread, a couple of tables and lamps, and a dark red upholstered chair wide enough for Alice to sit cross-legged on as she wrote up her day's notes.

The room had a clean modern bathroom. White tiled walls and floor, shower, no tub. No kitchen of her own, but that was fine. Alice had to share a small communal kitchen with other people in her section of the second floor, stocked with things like water and fruit and snacks and a self-serve coffee maker. There was a larger cafeteria elsewhere on the second floor where the Factory employed cooks to prepare simple, delicious meals.

Most mornings Alice grabbed a to-go cup of coffee and a piece of fruit. She didn't have time to sit and eat. She wasn't interested in making friends, like in the lunchroom at school. She had work to do. She woke up early, got going, got to it. Kept at it. A few breaks here and there, a little fresh air above ground, out in the cold of the winter mountains, but mostly she kept her head down and did what she did best.

Research. Meticulous, patient research. Searching. Finding.

Until recently, Alice Kern had been an analyst with a government division known simply as the Agency. No abbreviation, no initials like CIA, DIA, NSA.

Maybe she still was an analyst there. She wasn't certain of her current status. She hadn't communicated with anyone from her office for the past few weeks. It didn't seem safe to do it anymore. There might be people within the Agency who were trying to get her killed.

Alice had been working for the Agency for a little less than a year. She was twenty-six, just a few years out of college. She had a reason for joining the Agency. Her own reason.

Up until a few months ago, Alice had been conducting her work with quiet efficiency. No one noticed her, and that was by design. During the day she performed analysis on a wide variety of investigations conducted by field agents all over the world. She was a perfect fit for the work. Methodical, detail-oriented, dogged. Some people's personalities gave them infinite patience when dealing with tech support, or when cataloging baseball scores or some trivia near and dear to their hearts. Alice's patience found a different outlet.

At night, after work, she pursued her own private research project. It was the one topic that crowded out everything else in her life. And she would pursue it to the ends of the earth, if that was what it took. To the end of her life, if that was the price. She just hoped that the end of her life wasn't as soon as the people moving against her wanted to make it.

Alice was researching what happened to her parents. What *really* happened. Why. Who was behind it. Both her mother and father were murdered six years ago, when Alice was twenty and a junior in college. The police concluded it was just another random shooting into a crowd. Alice's parents were simply unlucky to be there along with the other victims.

But that explanation never satisfied her. Maybe she was fooling herself. Alice was willing to analyze her own motives, along with everyone else's. But if she wasn't fooling herself, if her parents were killed for some other reason besides just a madman's need to cause misery and death, then Alice knew she had the right analytical mind to help her uncover the truth.

She knew both of her parents would have done it in her place.

Her mother was an emergency room doctor. Dr. Aurora

Kern. Intelligent, inquisitive, full of imagination. Killed at the age of forty-seven. Alice's father, Will Kern, was a systems engineer who designed computer networks for companies in the San Diego area. Dead at forty-eight.

The two of them met during college when Will Kern started coming to the martial arts dojo run by Aurora's two older brothers. Aurora's parents had emigrated to California from the Philippines before Aurora was born. Her brothers were ten and twelve years older, respectively, and they had learned a particular Filipino style of martial arts as they were growing up. When Aurora was still just a little girl they started their own dojo in San Diego.

Aurora grew up fighting with her two brothers. She was small and scrappy and tough. And she was stealthy. They were bigger, but not always better. By the time Aurora was in college, she had earned a second-degree black belt and won numerous sparring competitions throughout the state.

But then came college. Aurora wanted to be a doctor. She started taking a heavy class load and didn't have time to train at the dojo as much as before. But she was an excellent instructor, especially of the new white belts, and her brothers talked her into still teaching for them a couple of nights a week.

And on one of those nights, Will Kern walked in.

He was tall, six-foot-three, fair-haired, and not too bad on the eyes. That's what Alice's mother said whenever Alice begged to hear the story again. Her mother was a foot shorter than the new white belt, but he was clumsy and had no skills. Aurora taught him how to safely take a fall, then she threw him. And threw him again.

"That's when I knew I loved her," Alice's father liked to claim.

But Alice's mother said it came a few weeks later, when she laid him flat with a backfist to the temple. Will Kern was supposed to block it. Aurora had been teaching him what to do. She broke him down with a groin shot that bent him at the waist. No point in reaching up to him when she could bring him down to her instead.

It looked like he was about to shift his torso and his hands exactly the way she showed him. He had better speed and coordination now than when he first came in, and should easily have blocked it.

But the way Alice's father told it, at the last possible second, he had been too distracted by the beauty of the face behind the fist.

Aurora had excellent control. She could place a high-speed punch within a hair of hitting her student and not actually make contact or hurt him. But Will lost his balance somehow and stumbled. All two hundred pounds of him came toppling forward and he drove his own temple hard into Aurora's sharp bony knuckles.

He fell like a tree, Alice's mother told her. Unconscious onto the mat.

Other people had been knocked out in the dojo before. Other students had missed blocking a strike. But Aurora didn't hold their heads on her lap and personally apply the ice packs her brothers kept in the freezer. She didn't offer to drive them home afterward under the guise of making sure they were okay. She didn't kiss anyone else she knocked out. Or decide to marry them a few months later.

Alice looked most like her mother. Small, dark, with long brown hair she usually wore in a ponytail. She fought like her mother, too. She trained in the same dojo and learned from her uncles and her mother. Learned from her father, too, who was reasonably proficient in martial arts by the time Alice came along.

She looked a little like him, too, people said. She had his same round Germanic face and cheeks. And her mother used to say that Alice smiled just like he did, even as a baby.

And why shouldn't Alice smile? Her life growing up had been wonderful. Loving parents, an easy time in school, the fun of growing up in her uncles' dojo. It was all fun. All play. No worries.

On nights when her mother worked the graveyard shift in the ER—a term Dr. Aurora Kern hated, since she worked hard never to have her patients end up in a grave—Alice and her father did projects together. For fun. Everything for fun.

They especially liked making models. Airplanes, castles, toy cars that would actually run. It was the kind of project that appealed to Alice's and her father's patient, meticulous personalities. They were never in a rush to finish. The fun was in figuring out how to put everything in its proper place.

And while they glued and fussed and pieced together all the hundreds of small components, Alice's father would teach her why each piece was necessary and how it made the whole object work. Houses and castles needed certain foundations and supports. Airplanes needed various aerodynamic features. Alice ate it all up. She loved that kind of intricate, deep-dive detail. Her father knew everything.

She could feel him sometimes now while she worked. While she tried to find out why he and her mother were dead. Alice could imagine him taking the time that she did, patiently unraveling layer after layer of lies and secrets and crimes. Not being in such a rush that some crucial piece was missed. If Alice missed it, her pursuit of the truth might all fall apart.

She had come to the Factory along with her friend Marnie Stemple seeking safety and sanctuary. The man who owned the Factory, retired Air Force Major Fritz Zimholt, had promised them a protected place to stay for as long as they needed it.

But it was his second promise that meant as much to Alice as the first: that she could have unlimited access to his computer database to continue her private research.

It was that research that had triggered an unexpected lethal response. Every time Alice logged into the Agency computer files, even remotely, she seemed to draw the assassins right to her. She still didn't know which particular rock she had overturned that was the vital one. But she was cut off now from continuing her research through the Agency. So Major Zimholt's offer to freely continue her search at the Factory had sealed Alice's agreement.

It was midday now, probably lunchtime for some people, but Alice had no appetite. She had slept a little in between quitting last night and starting up again this morning. If she was tired, she didn't care. She could sleep later, some day. Some day when she had all the answers.

She didn't have all the answers yet. Not even close. But she'd just found one. Or at least the faint trail that might lead her to one. She wasn't sure. For now she just stared at it on the screen in front of her. Her hands felt clammy. Her heart double-timed. Her brain said, *Alice, look.*

It was as though she had come upon just another nondescript door, nothing special about it, but she opened it just to be thorough.

She flipped on the light and stood on the threshold of a vast warehouse of information she never knew existed. There were so many new files, so many new leads to pursue, Alice might need ten or twenty more years to sift through them all.

Historical data. Current data. Some of it organized, but most of it not.

And there, like a small dusty box sitting on a warehouse shelf, sat a file that contained a familiar name.

William Konrad Kern.

Alice's murdered father.

2

The file Alice found was part of a hodgepodge collection of records, in a folder titled *NX35*. Those letters and numbers meant nothing to her.

She stumbled onto the folder late last night, and dutifully began opening the first several files. At least these had some organization. They were listed alphabetically. Alice began at the top with the A's.

Some of the files in the *NX35* folder contained just a few documents, some of them contained many. Alice scanned the various memos and reports, waiting for something to catch her eye, but nothing seemed especially intriguing. There were names and dates, but none of them meant anything to her. By the time she reached the end of the C's, Alice's eyelids were too heavy to hold open any longer. She gave up for the night and gave in to the overwhelming need to sleep.

This morning she started fresh with the D's. Kept

clicking and reading the files through E, F, G, and H. And then she came to a file called *Hecate*. She had never heard the word and didn't know what it meant. But she clicked it innocently. Her eyes immediately locked onto the familiar name.

And her heart stripped itself raw all over again.

Why was her father's name in the Factory's computer database? Not just his name, but specific dates and other information?

Alice stared at the computer screen for several long minutes, seeing the words and numbers after her father's name, but still not understanding what his name was doing there at all.

The bottom had dropped out of the room. Alice felt as if she were floating out in space with nothing solid to hold on to. She felt completely lost.

Lost, and betrayed.

There was no point in going to Major Zimholt to ask him what it all meant. He had lied to her so many times, right from the beginning.

Alice thought back to when she first met Major Fritz Zimholt, back at the military base known as Ultra.

He had treated her with such respect. He had been kind and forthcoming with information. And then he had sprung the most important information of all, that he had once served with Alice's grandfather Peter Kern some time during the Vietnam War. Alice knew her grandfather had been in the Army, not the Air Force like Major Zimholt. But Major Zimholt said the two of them had worked together, and Alice didn't press it any further at the time.

That connection to her Grandpa Peter meant something to Alice. She had loved her grandfather very much. He died when she was in high school, a few years before her parents were killed. Alice thought then that it was a kindness to her grandfather that he hadn't lived to grieve the terrible loss of his only son.

And Alice trusted Major Zimholt all the more because he spoke so highly of the grandfather she had loved.

But Major Zimholt was a liar.

Maybe he had lied about knowing Alice's grandfather, she wasn't sure now about that.

But she was absolutely certain that he had lied by pretending not to know Alice's father.

It was right there. Spelled out in the file. *William Konrad Kern, designer.* Konrad had been her grandfather's middle name, too. Spelled the German way, with a K.

After her father's name, Alice saw dates of employment that spanned twenty-six years. The same number of years she had been alive. But Will Kern's employment began six years before she was born and ended six years ago when he died. The record showed that he worked for Major Fritz Zimholt from the age of twenty-two until his death at age forty-eight.

Will Kern had already been working for Major Zimholt when he began courting pre-med student Aurora Catapang.

Alice stared at the computer screen and knew she was about to be sick. To see here in black letters on a screen that she didn't know her father at all.

But she didn't have the luxury of feeling sick. That

wouldn't get her anywhere. Alice's analytical mind finally kicked back into action again.

They had all lied to her. Not only Major Zimholt, but Alice's mother and father, too.

What did her father do for a living? He was a systems engineer. He worked for a company in San Diego. Alice had gone there to visit him many times.

A regular looking company. A nice reception area, a nice receptionist who knew Alice's name and always told her to go on up. Like there was nothing to hide. Everything out in the open. When Alice came to see her father, she didn't remember anyone suddenly exiting out of whatever was up on their computer screens, or quickly hiding papers underneath files, or behaving in any way other than could be expected from the kinds of men and women who made their living from designing software and computer networks. *Business solutions for business needs.* That was the motto written on the wall behind the receptionist's desk.

Bull. It was all bull.

Alice's father led a secret life.

And Alice's mother must have known. Dr. Aurora Kern was a bright, inquisitive woman. Will Kern couldn't have fooled her for long.

Although he had fooled Alice all her life. She thought of herself as bright and inquisitive, too. But it never occurred to her for even a minute that her father wasn't what he seemed.

Alice took her hands off the computer keyboard and folded them in her lap. She had to calm down. Her fingers were trembling. She could feel tremors all through her body.

What was true? What did she know for sure? Start there. Start somewhere.

Alice took a fresh breath. Closed her eyes and tilted her neck from side to side. She could hear it crack. She had been sitting too stiffly for too long.

What did she know for sure?

When she lived at home, before moving out for college, she saw her father leave the house around seven-thirty every morning, heading off to work.

To what work, she didn't know now. But she could count as a fact that he left.

Business trips: not a crazy amount of them, but some. Maybe once every two months, and gone for four or five days, maybe Sunday to Wednesday, Monday to Thursday.

Alice couldn't remember ever having an overnight sitter, so her parents must have coordinated Will's business trips with the days Aurora worked regular hours and not the graveyard shift.

But those were just the years Alice could remember. Who knew how they did it when she was a baby and a toddler.

Question: Did Aurora Kern know about her husband's work?

Answer: Unknown. Probably, but not for certain. Alice had to leave that question for another time. Guessing wasn't good enough. She needed actual facts.

Question: What did Will Kern do, exactly, for Major Zimholt? His employment record listed him as a designer. What exactly did that mean?

Alice had no idea. But she would investigate now to find out.

She didn't want to go straight to Major Zimholt. Couldn't just ask, *What did my father do for you? And why didn't you tell me he worked here? Why didn't you tell me you knew him?*

None of that. Because Major Zimholt could just lie to her again. And Alice wasn't interested in more lies. She had been wading through coverups and deceptions and secrets for the past year as she delved in the Agency's files. More lies didn't bring her any closer to finding out why her parents were dead. More lies were useless. Alice needed truth.

So she dragged her attention away from the paragraph about her father, and moved on to the person listed next in the *Hecate* file.

A name Alice recognized. A woman she had met. Not that long ago, on her first day at the Factory.

The woman had applied some kind of strange implement, shaped like a crude-looking metal gun, to the bullet hole in Major Zimholt's shoulder and to Marnie Stemple's broken ankle. Alice saw the glow of neon green light blasting out of the barrel.

Both injuries had been healed in an instant. Like a feat of magic. Like something out of a movie about wizards or strange aliens with miraculous powers.

And that had been Dr. Caroline Baird's explanation, when Alice had pressed her.

The pistol-shaped instrument was something Dr. Baird's father had found. At least that was what she said at first. But then she corrected herself.

It was given to him. By an alien.

Alice didn't believe it for a minute. It sounded like pure fantasy or science fiction. Alice enjoyed movies like that as much as anyone else. She could suspend her disbelief as heroes raced around in space blasting ray guns at alien enemies. But real life wasn't like that. And she resented someone trying to tell her something so obviously false. Better to say, *That's classified. I can't tell you.* Alice would have at least accepted that at the time and investigated it on her own some other way.

What surprised her about the answer was that Dr. Caroline Baird seemed like a normal, serious person. Major Zimholt had introduced her to Alice and Marnie as the Factory's chief scientist. She looked around her mid-fifties, average height, average weight, with shoulder-length gray hair and serious brown eyes behind her noticeably thick glasses.

But as soon as Dr. Baird pretended that her medical implement was something an alien gave her father, Alice's mind shut down. *Crazy. Case closed. Move on.*

There was no denying that the neon green light coming from the strange pistol had healed Marnie's and Major Zimholt's injuries. But Alice assumed there was a true explanation for the instrument, and she was simply being lied to, to cover it up. Some kind of advanced medical tech that wasn't known to the general public yet.

Alice had set aside Dr. Caroline Baird as an unreliable source from that minute on.

But now.

It was her name on the computer screen, directly beneath Alice's father's.

Dr. Baird's dates of employment extended longer than his by more than a decade. Began earlier and were still continuing now, six years past Will Kern's death.

Her job titles were different during different segments of time. Right now, Chief Scientist, just as Major Zimholt introduced her.

But almost thirty years ago she was responsible for something else.

Science advisor to William K. Kern, designer.

Dr. Caroline Baird had known Alice's father. She had worked with him, according to the records, for seven years.

And yet she had looked right into Alice's face and hadn't said a word about him. No, *Alice Kern? Will's daughter? I'm so happy to meet you. I knew your father well. What a loss. I'm so sorry.*

Nothing like that.

Alice copied down the information on her notepad. There wasn't a printer in here, and she didn't want anyone else in some central office to see what she printed out. She didn't want someone to report to Major Zimholt what she had found.

Alice closed out the file and clicked all the way to a fresh blank screen. Then she pushed back her chair and headed for the door.

She wasn't feeling sick to her stomach any more. Alice was fueled by a good strong case of rage.

3

Alice had some vague idea of where Dr. Baird's laboratory was. She had only been there once, but she remembered it being on the third floor and thought she knew which direction to take once she got down there.

There were no signs directing people where to go. You either knew or you didn't. You were escorted or you weren't. Alice took several wrong turns. She passed one of the third-floor kitchens, empty, and the larger cafeteria where a few people sat at tables enjoying sandwiches and some kind of hot meal the cooks had made. The only thing that tempted Alice was the smell of fresh coffee. But not tempted enough to take a detour. She needed to find the lab.

Finally Alice came to a familiar door. She tried to open it, but it was locked. There was a bluish-white lighted square like the one on Alice's bedroom door. A place to press a hand. It meant that no one could open the door unless their palm print was authorized.

Alice's wasn't.

She knocked. Pressed her ear against the door jamb. Heard nothing. Knocked again.

The door was thicker than she expected, because she didn't hear footsteps behind it. The door opened midway through her second knock.

Dr. Baird stood just inside. She looked harried. Irritated by the interruption.

But then her magnified eyes focused on Alice's face, and Dr. Baird softened.

"Alice, isn't it?"

"Alice Kern," Alice said. She resisted adding, *Cut the crap.*

"I'm right in the middle of something," Dr. Baird said.

"This won't take long," Alice said. She wasn't sure if that was true, but truth didn't seem to be important to people here.

Dr. Baird hesitated. But then she opened the door wider and let Alice inside.

The lab was about the size of a college classroom. Not one of the huge lecture halls, but one of the rooms where a teaching assistant might hold class. There were two long stainless steel counters running parallel the length of the room. Both had double sinks. There were instruments on top of the counters, microscopes, scales, the usual laboratory equipment. Alice didn't see the strange pistol Dr. Baird had used to heal Marnie and Major Zimholt. Alice remembered Dr. Baird using her handprint to unlock a steel cabinet in back to retrieve the pistol.

There were a few large whiteboards on the walls, filled with oversized handwritten notations. Considering the thickness of Dr. Baird's glasses, Alice guessed she needed to write in huge letters if she wanted to see them.

There was an institutional-looking desk in the back corner near the locked cabinet. It had battered metal legs and a yellowing Formica top. Not exactly top-of-the-line. But maybe it had already been in here when Dr. Baird first began working at the Factory, and she never bothered switching it out.

She didn't seem concerned with appearances. She wore baggy cotton drawstring pants with elastic at the bottoms, like a combination of sweat pants and scrubs. On top she wore a blue plaid flannel shirt over a plain white T-shirt. Not much different from the way Alice dressed as soon as she got home from work. The flannel shirt had splotches of white where bleach or some lab chemical had splashed on it.

On top of the institutional desk, hovering about six inches above the surface, were two large computer screens. Alice could see they were attached at opposite sides of the desk with two separate articulating arms. They reminded her the kind of adjustable mirrors she'd seen in hotel rooms. A person could swing the mirror out, forward, up or down, and angle it just perfectly so they could see.

Considering Dr. Baird's eyesight issues, Alice could imagine the scientist needed to be able to read her computer close up. Just having the screens on their factory-provided bases might not give her the flexibility she needed.

The size of the laboratory might provide a similar bene-fit. A larger lab could be hard to navigate through. Maybe everything Dr. Baird needed was close at hand.

Alice had done classwork in much larger labs during her

first three years of college. Multiple rows of tables, many sinks, plenty of room for a class of fifty to stand shoulder to shoulder at different stations and get their experiments done.

That time in her life felt ancient now. Just like her carefree, innocent childhood. Alice had started out pre-med, like her mother. But everything changed Alice's junior year. After her parents' murder, Alice stopped going to school for months. When she finally returned, becoming a doctor no longer felt important.

She started taking whatever classes she could find that might help her understand. Criminal psychology, forensics, cyber investigation, philosophy. The big picture and the narrow one. Good versus evil, and also how to grab fingerprints off of surfaces. The meaning of human existence, and how to interpret blood splatter patterns.

The floor had dropped out from under Alice then, too, and she was doing her best to rebuild it plank by plank even while she was trying to stand on it.

She finally settled on doing investigation via computer, rather than out in the field. Her brain worked that way. Just, she thought at the time, like her father's.

But now as Alice stood inside Dr. Caroline Baird's lab at the Factory, Alice thought of a different example her father set for her. His patient attention to detail while the two of them worked together building models. The way he taught Alice that they should assume every single piece, no matter how tiny, had to be necessary to make the whole object work. *If it came in the box, we need it.*

If Alice was ever going to find out why her parents were

killed, she needed every tiny piece of information she could find.

She had to assume Dr. Caroline Baird held some of those pieces.

Dr. Baird still stood just inside the doorway, back only far enough to have invited Alice in. Alice knew the tactic. Dr. Baird was signaling this interview would be short.

Alice saw no reason to be coy. If she wanted blunt truth, it was best to be blunt in her question.

"What is Hecate?" She pronounced it the way it was spelled, heck-ate.

Dr. Baird looked confused for a moment. Then she corrected the pronunciation. "Heck-a-tee. At least that's how he always pronounced it."

"My father."

Dr. Baird nodded.

For a brief few seconds the scientist stood stiff. Tense. Then her shoulders slumped. Dr. Baird let out a sigh. As though the idea of discussing the topic already tired her out. Or maybe it was an expression of relief. Alice didn't know.

"We might as well sit," said Dr. Baird. She motioned toward the desk in back. There was a hard metal chair to the right of it, for guests, Alice assumed, but not comfortable enough for them to want to settle in and stay too long.

Dr. Baird clearly wasn't on for chit chat. Alice didn't care. She wasn't feeling particularly polite. But for now she held off her questions and followed Dr. Baird to the desk in back.

"Coffee?" Dr. Baird asked.

"Actually, yes," Alice said.

Dr. Baird strung out the silence a little longer while she

refilled her coffee pot's reservoir and fiddled with the filter and grounds and got the coffee brewing.

Alice sat on the hard metal chair and waited. When the coffee was ready Dr. Baird poured it into two cups. "I don't have any sugar or cream."

"Don't need it," Alice said.

Dr. Baird finally settled onto her desk chair. It was more modern than Alice's or than the desk. A concession to ergonomics with its back and neck support.

Alice took a sip of coffee then began.

"You knew who I was," she said. "That first day I came here."

"Yes."

"Why didn't you say anything?"

Dr. Baird cupped her mug in her hands and let the steam fog up her glasses. It made them look like the milky eyes of a blind spider in a movie Alice once saw.

"I assumed he had his reasons," Dr. Baird said.

"Who?"

"Fritz. Major Zimholt. I could see he didn't want me to react."

Heat built up in Alice's blood. The more she thought about Major Zimholt's deception, the more enraged she felt.

Dr. Baird must have seen it, even though Alice was trying her best to remain calm.

"He wanted to know how good you are," said Dr. Baird. "How … similar to your father."

Alice forced herself to take another sip of coffee. To buy herself time. Not to just speak right away.

Her mind was busy, though. Analyzing exactly what Dr. Baird said. Trying to see it from her perspective.

"And you agreed," Alice said. "In all the time I've been here, you've never told me you knew him."

"But now I will," said Dr. Baird. "He was a wonderful boy. A wonderful man. I knew him a lot of years. As you probably know now."

Alice could feel the weight of her pain trying to take hold of her again. The sharp broken pieces of her anger pressing down on her patched over heart.

She didn't trust herself to speak. She simply nodded in response. And Dr. Baird took over from there.

"Project Hecate," she said. "You don't know the reference?"

Alice shook her head.

"Your father was very well-read."

Alice knew that. She rarely saw her father in the evenings without a book in his hand.

"Did you ever read *Macbeth*?" Dr. Baird asked.

"In high school," Alice said.

"Hecate was one of the three witches. *Double, double toil and trouble.*"

Alice didn't want to admit it, but she always thought the rhyme was *Bubble, bubble, boil and trouble.* Shakespeare never did much for her.

"Hecate was the chief witch," Dr. Baird said. "She has a much more important line later. The witches had given Macbeth a prophecy that he interpreted to mean he was immortal. Untouchable. He started making reckless decisions because he thought he couldn't lose.

"But Hecate told her fellow witches, *Security is mortals' chiefest enemy.* And she was right. Macbeth's overconfidence led to his downfall."

Dr. Baird leaned back in her chair and drank from her cup and watched Alice over the rim. She seemed to be waiting for some kind of reaction. Waiting for Alice to get it.

William Konrad Kern. Designer.

"He created some kind of security system for you," Alice guessed.

"For Major Zimholt," said Dr. Baird. "For this whole facility. It took years. Even though your father was brilliant at it. There were so many moving parts."

If it came in the box, we need it.

"Did my mother know?"

"Yes," Dr. Baird said.

Alice felt another unexpected stab of pain. So both of them had lied to her. All of her life. How was she supposed to feel about that?

"They both had the proper clearances," Dr. Baird said. "You must understand how secret the work is that we do here."

A new thought occurred to Alice. "Did my mother work for you, too?"

"Not us," Dr. Baird said. "But ... others."

Alice's head swirled. It was like stepping out of her childhood home and discovering they had lived on a different planet the whole time and she never knew.

She set down her cup of half-drunk coffee and leaned forward in her chair with elbows on her knees. She rested her forehead on her hands. The room was spinning slightly. She hadn't eaten for hours. She wasn't doing well.

"Is that…" The words choked in Alice's throat. She raised her head and looked into Dr. Baird's magnified brown eyes. "Is that why they were killed? Because of the work they both did?"

"We don't know," Dr. Baird said. "But of course we suspected it at the time."

"And since then?" Alice asked, the tension rising in her voice. She sat up straight again in the hard metal chair. "Has anyone been looking into it? Anyone besides me?"

"I don't know," Dr. Baird said. "I honestly don't. But I'm relieved to know you are. Your father…" Dr. Baird removed her thick glasses. She closed her eyes and massaged her fingers against her eyelids. She cleared her throat. She put her glasses back on. Then she leveled her gaze on Alice.

"Fritz—Major Zimholt—and I both loved your father as if he was our own son. You have to understand. We watched him grow up. He was just a young man when Fritz first recruited him. But he already showed such promise."

"I know he was smart," Alice said with a bite in her voice. She didn't need to hear how great her father was. She knew.

What she wanted were facts. Information. Leads. Truth. She could sit around and reminisce about her parents for the rest of her life, but it wouldn't get her any further in understanding why they were killed.

"So Hecate was, what, some computer program he designed? Some kind of security system?"

"More than that," Dr. Baird said. "It was a way of thinking. A way of forcing us to think. Even when he was young, he took charge. He always challenged Fritz about not getting too overconfident. Fritz already had security systems for every feature at the Factory. But Will showed us how inadequate they were. How easy to break. That's why it took so long. He would break things himself just so he could figure out how to put them back together better."

That was her father. The father Alice knew. The skeptic who didn't take anything at first glance. Who didn't just take things on faith. He needed proof. Alice could think of a hundred different incidences when her father showed that part of his personality.

It was Alice's personality, too. Her character. Maybe something she was born with. Just like her need for justice. Like her burning desire for good to always triumph over evil. Her mother could curl her tongue, Alice and her father couldn't. A matter of genetics. Maybe Alice came into this world wired to be more like her father, even though she looked like her mother. Maybe none of this was in her control.

It must be why she scoffed when Dr. Baird tried to tell her the instrument that had healed Marnie's ankle and Major Zimholt's shoulder had come from an alien. Ridiculous. Prove it. Convince me.

Dr. Baird must have tried to tell Will Kern things like that, too. Did he believe her at first? Did he believe her eventually?

There was no reason to wonder. Alice simply asked.

"Did my father believe in aliens?"

"Yes," Dr. Baird said, "he did."

"Did he have good reasons to?"

"Yes. He did."

Alice leaned back in her chair. She felt tired. Tired and hungry and confused.

"Did my mother?" she asked, although she could already guess the answer. Dr. Aurora Kern always had a more accepting imagination.

"She did," said Dr. Baird. "And yes, she had good reasons, too."

Alice nodded. She was almost out of gas.

"Tell me again," Alice said. "Security…"

"Is mortals' chiefest enemy," Dr. Baird finished. "It was why Will said we could never let down our guard. We might think we had things locked down here as well as possible, but he was always finding faults with it. He was always looking for a better solution."

"And he was still working for you when … when they died?"

"I was expecting to see him just a few weeks after."

Dr. Baird gazed at Alice with sympathy. With shared regret. That Will Kern had exited both their lives so suddenly and tragically.

"Did you ever meet my mother?" Alice asked.

"No," Dr. Baird said. "I'm afraid I never had the pleasure."

"Did he … talk about us?" Alice asked. Her voice felt small and childlike. It was a childish wish. She didn't mean to expose it.

"He was … careful," Dr. Baird said. "He set the example for all of us. The more people who knew things, the more exposed we all were. So I knew he had a daughter. I knew when you were born. But I didn't know your name. Not until I met you."

Alice nodded. She felt empty. She wished Dr. Baird had said, *He talked about you all the time! He loved you so much.*

But it was just one more piece in the new puzzle that confronted her. The father she thought she knew, but she really didn't.

The mother she thought she knew, but really didn't.

"I think you should talk to Fritz if you want to know any more," said Dr. Baird. She stood up from her chair. She was obviously done.

But Alice stayed seated. She wasn't ready to leave. She wasn't ready to stop asking questions.

"What … what am I supposed to do here?" she asked. She tilted her head back and looked up at Dr. Baird. "Why did Major Zimholt ask me to come?"

Dr. Caroline Baird lifted her head, too, and looked up at the wall where it met the ceiling. As if searching there for inspiration.

"I think … we owe you something. Just as we owed him. He was…" She gazed back down at Alice. "Truly one of a kind."

Now Alice rose to her feet, too. She and Dr. Baird stood apart for a moment, just letting the import of their conversation settle. Alice felt like they had only just begun to explore the topic. Maybe Dr. Baird thought this was the end of it. Alice didn't know.

"Will he … do you think Major Zimholt will tell me the truth if I ask?"

"As much as he can," Dr. Baird said. "Yes."

"Why didn't he tell me any of this before? Back when he first met me?"

Dr. Baird smiled. "Security … et cetera."

"So he didn't trust me," Alice said.

"We've been trained not to trust anyone. Not until we have a better sense of who they are." Dr. Baird made a gesture, an *on the other hand...* "And I suppose he also wanted to put you through your paces, to see if you were any match for your father. I can tell you that finding the Hecate file isn't something that many people can do. It was a maze within a maze within a maze. You must have noticed that."

"I did," Alice said. "So my father created that?"

Dr. Baird nodded. "You bet he did."

"Are there … other things here that I'm supposed to figure out? Why, just to prove myself?" She could feel a flash of anger again, flaring up.

She didn't owe it to Major Zimholt or Dr. Baird or anyone else to prove that she might be as clever as her father.

Alice wasn't sure she was, anyway. Nothing to prove. She could admire him without feeling she had to top him.

"So why am I here?" Alice asked again.

"Maybe the same reason I am," said Dr. Baird. "Because of our fathers. Because they started something they couldn't finish."

But before Alice could ask her any questions about that, Dr. Baird hustled her toward the door.

"Never enough time," said Dr. Baird. "That was another quote your father taught me. Something else from Shakespeare, but I don't know which play. *I wasted time and now time doth waste me.* I'm always behind, Alice. Years and years behind."

Alice paused at the door and held out her hand. Dr. Baird took it and clasped it in her warm, rough hand.

"I'm not done," Alice said. "I need to know everything now. I hope you'll help me, Dr. Baird."

"Caroline," she said. "Your father called me Caroline, too. Go talk to Fritz first. I have to get back to my work now. Goodbye, Alice. Good luck."

Alice heard the door lock behind her. She stood for a moment in the hallway, regaining her bearings.

There was no one around. As she walked past the cafeteria she saw it was empty again. People were busy here. No one just sat around and lingered.

She needed food. Fresh air. A fresh mind to process all she had learned. She didn't feel angry anymore, just tired.

But she wasn't confused anymore, either. Alice might still be far from finding all the answers, but she knew more now than she had known in the past six years, since her parents were killed. More than in the past twenty-six years, since she was born.

She had found a brand new box of parts, to build a brand new model of the world. Her world, her family's world, the world of this place she had come to, the Factory, believing it was random.

None of it was random. Including her parents' death. Alice knew that to the base of her bones.

But now her search had led her further than she had ever gotten before. That counted for something. And she would keep searching, until she found the whole truth.

She might not know Shakespeare, but Alice knew another quote instead. From one of the fantasy books her father gave her when she was a child.

The best finders are the seekers. If you want to find something, you should look for it.

People were all the same. They were born to be who they were. The same for Alice, for her parents, probably all the way back to the cavemen.

Good, evil. Kind, cruel. Curious, complacent. It was in their character. Alice still believed that. She knew that her parents were good people, brave and honest and kind, even though they had lied to her all her life. Even though Alice no longer knew what was true. She still believed in Will and Aurora Kern.

The truth was out there, even if it was going to be hard for Alice to find. Even if it was hidden inside a maze within a maze and another maze.

Alice knew she had been born a seeker. And she had in mind where she would look next.

CONTROL

1

In the rain Julie can't quite make out the skin color of the creatures she sees watching her from between the trees, but they look slightly peach. That's good. It means they're juveniles. Not yet skilled at the hunt. It's the dark burnt orange ones, the adults, that Julie has to keep ahead of. They're busy now, tearing, ripping, eating—but for how long? She keeps on running. Hard.

It's mid-July, but up this high in the Wind River Mountain Range in Wyoming, above eleven thousand feet, it's as if it's early spring. The pale green grass coming up on the meadow is slick beneath Julie's boots. Until the rain, the day was warm and fresh and the woods smelled like pine.

Then everything went to hell.

Julie finishes racing across the meadow and hits the game trail just inside the woods. It threads her between tree trunks, the pine and fir and spruce, and she has to hop over fallen logs and thick exposed roots, all of them slowing her down.

The meadow was fast and easy in comparison. But also entirely exposed.

Not that they can't find her here, even in dense woods. Julie has no illusions. Her only hope is to stay out in front of them.

The footing on the game train is tricky. Deer have smaller, more nimble hooves. But Julie's boots are new, with maximum tread, and they fit well so her feet aren't sloshing around inside them, throwing her off balance.

She keeps the hood of her raincoat down so she can hear. How much time would she have even if she did hear them first? The crack of a twig, the swish of their clawed feet on wet grass or damp soil—she could react in a split second and they'd still get her. After what she just saw, there's no question of that.

Julie is fit and strong. She's twenty-eight. She lives at altitude, she hikes mountains like this all time, so it's not the steepness of the slope or the altitude making her heart scream the way it is. It's fear. Pure, justified fear. But it's doing more than its evolutionary job and is currently overloading Julie's circuits. Trying to misfire her brain into thinking it's too late, this won't work, just give up. It's over.

It's not over. As long as she's alive she has hope. Julie shoves down the fear. It's not helping her. It's not motivating her to move any faster. She's already running as hard as she can, tearing across the muddy forest floor in the rain, making the calculations in her head.

The helicopter is somewhere between five and six miles

away. Just waiting for Julie to return with the other four members of her party.

Just Julie now, if she makes it. Party of one.

The creatures might be a mile behind her now. Maybe. Depending on how fast they eat. Depending on whether any of the adults noticed they let one get away.

Would the juveniles be able to tell them? They must have some way of communicating. *Papa, I saw one! She went that way. I'm hungry...*

Five to six miles to the helicopter, maybe two miles an hour in wooded terrain, faster in the open meadows. Somewhere in between across stretches of solid rock.

Say two hours. Three. She can't run at this pace for three.

But maybe the creatures can. Julie doesn't know. Finding out more about them was the whole point of this expedition.

At least Julie knows one thing for sure now: How they tear their prey apart.

Whether she'll get a chance to tell anyone remains to be seen.

2

Tim Cudahey checks the figures on his computer. Checks again.

Stalling.

He looks around at the other Control engineers sitting at their desks. Thirty-nine of them, all hunched over their computers, just like Tim, engineer number forty.

They're in a bunker, of sorts, known to insiders as the Tunnels. Lots of different concrete-walled rooms and passageways exploiting a cave system that already existed inside a mountain in Montana.

The room where Tim and the other Control engineers work is long and narrow and dimly lit, with most of the light coming from their generously-sized computer screens. The forty engineers all sit at their individual stations along one continuous work table, like factory workers standing next to each other in front of an assembly line.

It's like a casino in Vegas, the way they keep the lights in here. Tim has never been to Vegas, but he's read about it. The casino guests never know whether it's day or night, bright or dark, raining, not raining, hot or cold. Uniform temperature, everything the same, all the time. That way they don't realize it's time to leave.

When did Tim last sleep? A day ago? That feels artificial, too. The way you walk into the next room, stretch out on one of the soft narrow couches, put on your noise-cancelling headphones and the black padded eyeshades and you sleep when you're tired (exhausted) and wake when you're awake. Then back to the computer, continue your work.

Six weeks like this, that's a shift. Then you go out into the real world again, it feels completely unreal, and you're in bright loud grocery stores or hot loud parking lots or cold loud crowds.

Personal life? Maybe. If your girlfriend is still there and hasn't left you like any of the other engineers' girlfriends or boyfriends because this whole lifestyle is too weird.

I can't call you or text you?

No.

What if something happens?

No.

What if there's an emergency?

You'll have to handle it yourself.

A few of the engineers on this shift are married, amazingly. But almost everyone else is single. Even the two engineers at the Tunnels who are married to each other have to work different shifts and hardly see each other at all.

Tim thinks about Julie Trident a *lot*.

She is not his girlfriend. In what kind of world would she ever look at him? His pale skin, ginger hair, unimpressive body, nothing at all to recommend him physically or even intellectually compared to some other people. He's got nothing.

Whereas Julie.

Twenty-eight years old, five-foot-seven, shoulder-length brown hair she always wears in a low ponytail against her neck, slim, tough, more mannish than Tim is, if he has to be honest. She's killed aliens, lots of them, and from their conversations about it afterward, it never seems to bother her, she understands her mission.

Spare the Greys. Always. They're the "good" aliens.

Take out the LPs. He hates to call them by their full name, it's so cartoonish. Back in the day, before Tim was even born, the LPs had a more respectable, scientific designation. RL-40s, whatever that meant. But it's no secret what everyone calls them now. Lizard People. The bad aliens.

Adults seven-feet tall, youngsters about six-foot. Rough skin like an iguana. Dark brown, some of them burnt orange. The young ones coral-colored or peach. Reptilian eyes, vertical slits with black pupils. Iguana-like heads, broad at the top, tapering down at the nose, two vertical nostrils with highly acute smell. Thick black tongues they stick out when they're about to attack. Like a kid concentrating on his math homework, tongue sticking partway between his teeth, not even aware of it.

Tim has seen autopsy photos of them and the footage from Julie Trident's memories. Horrid.

"Cudahey?"

"Sir."

The Control shift supervisor, Randy Mitchell, makes his rounds every two hours, which is the only way Tim knows two hours have passed. It could have been minutes as far as he knew.

Randy Mitchell is even paler than Tim, as though he hasn't been outside the Tunnels for a decade. Maybe he hasn't. He somewhere in his fifties. His hair is nearly gone. He's soft and pudgy, with soft pudgy hands. He bites his nails down to the quick. Tim can see it whenever Randy points at his screen. But the supervisor is smart and capable and respected by the engineers. He used to do their job a longer longer than they have, and he has an instinct for knowing what they might be missing.

"You got Trident?" Randy Mitchell asks.

"Yes, sir." Tim points at his computer screen. "Flying back to Wyoming base."

It took three hours and twenty minutes, but Julie Trident finally made her way back to the stealth helicopter parked and waiting for her down the mountain.

"Casualties?"

"At least four," Tim says. He watched each of their white dots on the screen disappear, one by one. He held his breath, sick inside, afraid for Julie Trident.

"Damn."

"Yes, sir," Tim says.

Randy Mitchell moves on to other engineers and asks for updates from their sectors.

Tim stares at the screen again. Checks the figures again.

Julie is hurt. He's waiting for her to check in, give him

voice confirmation, but he can see from the numbers that her heart and respiration rates are both elevated, which shouldn't be happening at all anymore this long after the attack.

He's kept charts on her for the past two years. He knows her stats like a baseball nut knows his players. He knows what she's like. She can take pressure like no one else. She reacts, sure, her body isn't a machine, but after it's over everything calms right down.

About eighteen months ago she got sliced, right down the length of her thigh, and Tim knew about it days before she called in and told anyone. By then it was blazing hot with an infection she somehow thought she could handle on her own. But the infection got the better of her and Julie passed out somewhere in the wilderness. She was unconscious off and on for two days, getting sicker by the hour. The LPs could have tracked her and killed her. But even sick, Julie had found a safe place to hide before passing out.

Tim watched her numbers climb. He knew she was in trouble. He would have sent a rescue chopper for her if he could. But he wasn't supposed to know any of it.

It's just that he's written a special program that helps him keep a closer watch.

It's not sneaky. Not really. Just ingenious. It's math. It's cross-scoring various data points that he's accessing from places he shouldn't really have clearance for, but Randy Mitchell's predecessor wanted someone to keep special track of Julie Trident, and Tim Cudahey was lucky enough to get the job.

It's why he volunteers for extra shifts.

If Julie Trident is working out in the field somewhere, he wants to be here for her. So he works six weeks, takes off two, comes back for the next six. Everyone else does six on, six off. If he could take off just a week in between he would do it, but that's against the rules.

It's no wonder he can't keep a girlfriend. He isn't that special. No one would want him or this life.

Tim hears the heavy, reinforced door of the Control room make a slight sucking noise as it closes tight. The supervisor is gone.

He goes back to looking at Julie Trident's vitals. Her heart is still elevated. Something is definitely wrong.

3

Julie stares out the window of the helicopter. It's a new model, stealth technology, eerily quiet, with retractable rotor blades like the kind of ceiling fan that tucks back up above its light fixture.

The pilot of the helicopter is new to her, but she's seen the co-pilot before. Gardner, she thinks his name is. She won't ask. She doesn't want to talk to either of them.

There's a tremor in her right arm. She keeps trying to still it, use sheer will to make it settle, but there's something neurological going on and that's that.

Julie closes her eyes. Ignores the tremor and focuses on her brain.

Her mentor, Colonel Jenks, taught her a skill back in advanced training three years ago. At first every time she did it she felt a kind of mental nausea, like her mind wanted to vomit, even though her body felt fine.

It was a way to store away certain memories. Certain connections and ideas that Julie can come back to later when the stress of the event has passed and she's ready to start making sense of it and planning for her next excursion with the new knowledge to guide her.

She visualizes her brain in its two halves, left and right.

She can feel where her memories are, lower left, back behind her left ear.

She copies them, like copying a computer file or a digital photo.

She mentally drags the copy over to the right side of her brain. Across the mental divide to a place where she can hide it from the people who will want to access it and maybe delete it later.

She stores her memories in what formerly felt like a dead space on the back of the right side of her head. Halfway between her right ear and the midpoint of the back of her skull.

Tim Cudahey back in Control knows where it is. He told her so. It felt like a violation at first, but then he explained why it was to her advantage that he knew, and that the two of them would have to keep it a secret from everybody else.

"Colonel Jenks sent me," he told her.

Colonel Jenks was now dead.

Killed in action on a mission Julie vaguely remembered being involved in, but the memories were too wispy to grab on to.

Back then she was still having trouble nailing down the skill of searching for certain moments inside her brain and reviewing them whenever she needed to. Once Colonel Jenks died, Julie's progress abruptly stopped.

Then one day she heard a voice inside her head, telling her his name was Tim Cudahey and he was there for her. That he would be monitoring her and helping her from then on.

She has never met him in person. As far as she knows.

Sitting in the helicopter now with her eyes closed, Julie copies her memories to the right side. Then she mentally brushes away the traces of what she did, like someone using a cluster of foliage to flurry up the dirt behind them and erase any proof of their footsteps.

It hurts a little, holding both files in their two distinct places. It's still unnatural, no matter how many times she's done it. She'll feel this way until Control takes the memories from the left side of her brain some night in the future while she sleeps.

It's happened enough now, she's learned to recognize the signs. She'll wake up feeling mentally lighter. There'll be a strange kind of slickness to her thoughts, like when she first got her braces off in high school and felt her tongue slick across her bare teeth.

At some point she'll have a conversation with Tim Cudahey, however he's managing that. She doesn't know and isn't sure she wants to.

The first time they talked, not in voices, but inside her brain, he gave her a few facts that no one else had ever told her.

He told her to store this conversation away on the dark

right side of her brain, like a transcript from a chat she might have with tech support.

"They have more control than you know," he told her two years ago when she awoke in the infirmary with his words inside her brain. "It's part of the general overall agreement you sign. It's hidden in there, your compliance."

She started to speak out loud. She still felt fuzzy from the pain killers. "What are you talking about?"

He shushed her inside her head. "Just here," he said. "I can hear you. You don't have to talk out loud."

She dropped back onto the stiff white sheets on the infirmary bed and gently lowered her head back down to the pillow. Tim Cudahey's voice in her mind felt heavy. An extra burden she wasn't ready to carry.

"Like this?" she thought to him.

"Exactly. How are you?"

She licked her dry lips. "Thirsty."

"Sit up," Tim told her. "Drink something. I need you to be alert and focused."

There were other times, since then, when he seemed to be able to feel the state of her mind. *You need coffee... You need to eat something... I'll wait, then we'll talk.*

The first time, he took it slowly.

By the end of it, maybe half an hour before she was too exhausted to listen inside her head anymore, she knew the basics of what he was trying to tell her.

It had been going on for decades, since at least the Apollo space program in the 1960s, maybe before. A way of capturing and then erasing certain memories, while leaving other ones intact. A very precise excision of exactly the information certain members in power didn't want the astronauts or other key players in the military or government to be able to share with the wider world.

"Have you ever heard the astronauts talk about it?" Tim Cudahey asked her. "Their experiences on the moon?"

"I'm … not sure," she thought back.

"There are missing sections of time. Or missing details. Maybe they remember turning in a certain direction and looking up, but then what they saw is gone from their minds. Next thing they know, they're looking in a different direction, maybe three minutes later, and their memories pick up again."

"Why?" Julie asked him. "What aren't they supposed to remember?"

"What they found," Tim said. "There were already structures on the moon when they got there. Massive glass domes and towers and tunnels. Advanced engineering. Intricate designs. All of it built and abandoned by some other more advanced civilization. An *alien* civilization. Maybe as long as a thousand years ago."

"Come on," Julie said. The story was getting out of hand. Granted, it was happening inside her head, which was some kind of advanced biological engineering all its own, but this Tim Cudahey, whoever he was, was obviously a rabid conspiracy theorist.

"The government would never be able to hide something like that," Julie thought at him. "There must be thousands of photos of the moon—"

"Altered," Tim said. "Negatives hand-painted black.

Images distorted. Astronauts instructed to aim their cameras anywhere but toward the structures."

"And you're saying they don't remember that," Julie said, still unconvinced.

"There are things *you* don't remember," Tim told her. "They've been removed from your brain. We're very good at it. I can give you a whole list."

Julie still remembers what it felt like to hear that. A cold wave seemed to wash through her veins. The pain pills made it hard to think as clearly as she wanted to, and she wanted to tell Tim Cudahey no, that was impossible.

But was it?

She could remember a few times lately when her memories from one of her missions felt … off. Like a word on the tip of your brain that you keep trying to call up, but it just won't come.

It had happened most recently after an excursion into the Idaho wilderness. She set out with two other scientists and a guard to examine an area in the Sawtooths. A scout doing air reconnaissance thought he saw a group of Greys. The good aliens. The ones who were no threat.

Julie could have sworn the guard with them got hurt during their mission, but she couldn't remember any of the details. She wrote out her report afterward and had to leave that part of it vague.

She thought she remembered blood, but that was all.

At the time she assumed she was just tired or still wrestling with the effects of a few too many nights sleeping at high altitude.

But what if it was something else? What if Tim Cudahey was telling her the truth?

"But why would they do that?" Julie asked him. "To the astronauts or any of us?"

"Because we're all tools to be used," Tim said. "Ways of bringing in data. But none of us personally matter. I hate to say it, but we're all disposable."

He gave her another few examples, examples she stored away in her secret vault, and ever since then Tim has helped her hide away what she sees during her excursions so she can continue to have enough information to help her survive.

He's also helped her learn to access those hidden memories, to be able to search among all of them for patterns that might not otherwise be apparent in the moment.

Maybe the four people Julie watched being ripped apart by the LPs today had as much knowledge and experience as she did.

But maybe they all forgot it.

Maybe those memories, for whatever reason, had been removed by Control.

Julie thinks about how slow they all were to react. Two other field biologists, like her, and two well-armed military escorts.

They had all received the same briefing, they all knew what danger signs to be alert for, but Julie was the only one who realized they were about to be attacked.

The others continued doing what they were doing, even though Julie shouted at the scientists to run. Even though she pointed out the movement in the trees and yelled at the guards to shoot.

Maybe in the rain none of them could hear her. But she doesn't really believe that.

She thinks it was something else.

The way one of the biologists, Dr. Virginia Ash, just looked at Julie with a kind of dreamy expression in her eyes.

Not afraid. Dr. Ash should have been afraid.

Julie's own reaction time has improved steadily in the past two years. In part because in the beginning after Tim first contacted her, she could sometimes hear him inside her head shouting, *"RUN! YOU HAVE TO GO!"*

The LPs were so fast. Lithe and fluid and it was over before the others even moved.

Screaming, snarling, the sucking sounds of limbs detached at the joints. More screams. Then silence. Silent except for the beating rain and the audible pounding of Julie's heart.

They ate her colleagues like beach picnickers sucking meat from lobster legs.

Clothes discarded. Hair and skin and bones discarded. Just the tender insides that the LPs have learned to love.

Julie saw more of the LPs, the younger, peach-colored ones, but though they watched their elders with palpable hunger and longing, Julie knew they didn't have the skills or maybe the bodily anatomy yet to join in themselves. The younger ones would get it through regurgitation from the adults, straight down their throats.

But they could have chased her. They had the same long legs and presumably the same alarming speed. But maybe they were too mesmerized by the feast in progress to notice one of the humans getting away.

Or maybe she's wrong about that. Julie will have to detail it out in her report. Maybe other people in the field have noticed the same thing. They're learning about this worst of the alien species, it seems, one horrifying encounter at a time.

4

Tim Cudahey waits until Julie Trident's vitals settle down.

Then he opens a communication line in their minds.

"Are you all right?"

"Right arm," Julie thinks back at him. "It's still shaking. I don't know what's wrong. No obvious injury."

"Did any of them touch you?" he asks.

"No. I got away clean."

"Any of their fluids, anything?" Tim asks.

"No."

Tim sits back in his black ergonomically-designed desk chair and thinks on his own, away from Julie's mind.

"Do you have full sensation, all five fingers?" he asks her.

He can picture her flexing her strong, tan hand.

"Some tingling overall," she answers. "Weakness in the last two fingers."

"Swelling?" Tim asks.

"Slight."

"Place your hand against your heart," he says.

He taps out a special command to analyze the overlaying appendage in addition to her heart rate. The blood flow is compromised. He can see the result, though not the cause.

"Keep it elevated," he says. "Tell the pilot to take you to the Factory, not base. Get medical help there as soon as you can."

"All right," Julie says. "Now go look. Talk to me when you're done."

Tim glances around the Control room. No one is paying attention to him. They never do. He isn't sure how much time had elapsed. There are no clocks in here. He might have five minutes before Randy Mitchell comes back to check on all of them, or he might still have an hour.

The problem with watching Julie's memories is that he knows they will be immersive. It will be hard for him to disengage if he suddenly realizes Randy Mitchell is looking over his shoulder.

"I have to wait for the next cycle," he tells her.

"I'm going to try to sleep," she tells him.

He can picture that too.

Also too immersive.

5

The helicopter lands at a small airport in the Wasatch Mountain Range in Utah where Julie has been several times before. The pilot and co-pilot go one way, Julie goes another.

This is the Factory, a kind of private base operated by a military contractor, Retired Air Force Major Fritz Zimholt. Julie has met Major Zimholt a few times. He reminds her of her own badass grandfather, proud U.S. Marine, solid and dependable and unfortunately long departed.

The facility is mostly underground, built deep into the excavated hillside. The airport up top that's visible to the world looks like one of those upscale regional airports that rich people fly into for their ski vacations and to spend the weekend at their mountain mansions.

But down below are the real works. An industrial warren where a wide variety of specialized aircraft and equipment are made.

Julie hurries down the long span of metal stairs toward the immense and brightly-lit hangar down below. Concrete hallways and more metal stairways will take her down two more levels to the infirmary.

She cradles her right arm with her left. The arm has gotten weaker during the flight from Wyoming. It's enough of a concern now that she rushes past the places where she'd normally pause, stick her head in, see if anybody she knows is here today.

At the infirmary she's taken right in, screened off behind a curtain, and a nurse helps her remove her shirt. Her right arm is shaking worse now. Julie can't pretend she's not worried.

"Clearance?" she asks the doctor, a woman in her forties with chin-length salt and pepper hair. Julie has never had a reason to be in the infirmary here before and has never met any of the medical staff.

The doctor shows her ID. Dr. Roberta Tognocci. Her clearance is high enough.

"LP attack," Julie tells her. "Killed four of my people. They never touched me, but something obviously happened."

Dr. Tognocci takes Julie's arm in her hands and begins gently manipulating it, extending and rotating it.

"Any pain?" Dr. Tognocci asks.

"No, it's more a vibration. Like there's a tuning fork right against my bones."

Dr. Tognocci holds Julie's arm in her right hand, and presses her left thumb deep into the base of Julie's neck where a tight band of tendons connects to her shoulder.

The vibration stops.

Dr. Tognocci removes her thumb. The vibration kicks in again.

Julie reports both.

Dr. Tognocci asks her nurse for a medication of some kind. It comes in the form of a large needle.

Julie curses.

The doctor smiles. "I know. But it works. Hold on."

With her good hand Julie catches Dr. Tognocci's wrist before the doctor can administer the shot. "Tell me what's in this first," Julie says. "I'm a biologist. Go ahead and get technical."

Dr. Tognocci lists all the ingredients. "It's a nerve-blocker we've come up with. So far it does the job."

The pain of the needle is worth it, even though Dr. Tognocci shoots it right into Julie's neck. The vibration stops almost immediately.

Julie can feel her muscles relax for the first time in hours.

"What caused it?" she asks the doctor.

"Something new," Dr. Tognocci says. "From what we can tell, the LPs have weaponized their scent. It wasn't like this a few months ago."

"Even in the rain?" Julie asks.

"Evidentally."

Julie shakes her head. "Evolution."

"Not just for Earthlings," Dr. Tognocci agrees.

6

Tim waits for Randy Mitchell to finish his rounds.

"Trident?" Mitchell asks.

"Stable," Tim reports.

Then the quiet, heavy door seals closed once more and Tim now has plenty of time.

He accesses Julie's memories.

He prefers to work with the original file still on the left side of her brain. He can work off the copy if he has to, but sometimes the original has just slightly clearer resolution.

And sometimes, he suspects, Julie unconsciously edits her memories as she moves them to the safe repository over on the right.

She dampens the fear. It's natural. The mind doesn't want to remember how terrified it felt, in the same way the body won't save a crisp, clear memory of pain. It generalizes.

It's a survival mechanism. It was something studied extensively with burn victims. The agony is so unbearably intense, the mind places a kind of filter over it, capping how much pain it will allow itself to remember.

Tim learned all about it from Colonel Jenks, the mentor Tim once shared with Julie Trident.

He's never told her that. Colonel Jenks ordered him not to.

Tim taps out his series of commands, and there he is, where Julie was the moment her brain alerted her that something was dangerously wrong.

He can smell them in her memory. The LPs give off a fetid kind of stench. The closest Tim can come, although he'd never tell this to anyone else, is the sour, pungent smell on your finger after you've dug inside your own belly button.

Or it's like the smell of underwear after you've been wearing it for several days, sweating in it, not properly cleaning yourself.

The few times he's discussed it with Julie, he doesn't describe it either way. He just calls it *musky*.

Julie calls it *the funk*.

But that's as light-hearted as they get. Because the LPs are deadly serious, and Julie is brave, but she's not reckless. She's never been one to joke around like some of her colleagues after the fact. Tim gets it—they survived, they're relieved to be alive—but some of the braggadocio ("Kicked some lizard *ass!*") only highlights how scared they really were at the time.

Julie doesn't pretend she's never afraid. That's one of the many things Tim likes about her.

He watches two different streams of information during

this memory: what he can see, feel, hear, touch, and taste from Julie's perspective, and what the computer can show him about her vitals in each moment.

Her heart rate and respiration were normal right up to now. But there's a spike in both. She knows something is wrong.

He sees through her eyes as she scans the thick conifer forest all around her. It's raining heavily, one of those typical July thunderstorms that blankets the mountains every afternoon. Whatever sunlight had been poking through the high canopy of fir and spruce and pine is now dimmed down to a gray unfriendly light that feels more like evening than afternoon.

Even in the rain Tim can smell the familiar sharp scent of the pine trees.

But on top of that he catches a whiff of musk. *The funk.*

Julie smells it, too.

She strains to listen. All Tim can hear are a few birds still chirping despite the downpour, and the low conversation being carried on by the two scientists Julie has led out there.

Dr. Virginia Ash, thirty-two, short and sturdy-looking and intensely smart from what Julie has seen, and Dr. Jason Maldridge, forty-six, a little too condescending for Julie's taste, but she's just the guide, she doesn't really care. Her assignment is to bring the scientists out to this section of forest where scouts saw some evidence of alien habitation. Whether it's the peaceful Greys or violent LPs, the scouts didn't know.

Julie knows these mountains. She's spent considerable

time since her teenage years roaming a variety of mountains in the west. Her specialty, before the alien incursion, was animal predators found at elevations above eight thousand feet.

Because of the question about which alien species they might find on this particular mission, the powers that be have assigned two soldiers to guard Julie and the other two biologists. The soldiers carry automatic rifles with special pulse beams. Julie carries her own firearm, an automatic pistol that Colonel Jenks gave to her when she completed his advanced training.

The soldiers stand guard near the three scientists, rifles at the ready, alert.

Doctors Ash and Maldrige are crouched on the ground, examining something in the mud, murmuring to each other about it.

Julie isn't watching them. She's scanning the woods. Her heart rate is elevated. She's holding her breath.

Suddenly she shouts, "THERE!"

Tim sees it too: movement off to their left.

Julie points to it for the soldiers, then grabs Dr. Ash's arm and tries to yank her to her feet.

Dr. Ash resists. She looks confused. And a little irritated about the interruption.

Dr. Maldridge looks around him, alarmed, but he's still crouched on the soggy ground.

"NOW!" Julie yells at the scientists. "RUN!"

She takes off to her right, setting the example. They all went through this in the briefing the day before. If she said to run, they were supposed to run. No questions asked, just do it and do it now.

Behind her Julie can hear a sound come crashing through the trees. Then shouts and the rain-dampened stutter of rifle fire.

Julie races away. She hopes to hear at least two sets of boots pounding across the wet forest floor behind her.

She's learned to run fast and keep running. Don't hesitate, don't look back. It's the only way.

She hears screams. The squelching. The sickening sounds of the attack.

Don't do it, Tim thinks. *Please don't.*

It's involuntary, only because he doesn't want to see.

But of course Julie Trident has to look. She's gathering data. She's a tool.

Some of Tim's colleagues don't mind the gore. Some of them enjoy it. He's sat through briefings with some of his fellow Control engineers where they've actually applauded some of the bloodiest memories.

Tim isn't supposed to be watching Julie Trident's memory on his own, before his supervisors have filtered it. But he's seen them fake some of her footage before, and he's learned his lesson.

He watches, as Julie watched from what felt like a safe distance as the LPs ripped apart and savaged the four humans.

Julie's heart rate is racing. There's a sour, rancid taste in her mouth. Like breathing in some toxic fume that then spreads out over her tongue.

She's trying to keep her breath quiet, even though it's

rapid and ragged. She's seen the young ones, the peach-colored ones, watching from a nearby stand of trees, and Julie doesn't want to alert them to her presence.

Even the young ones are taller than she is by at least half a foot. They have the same thin, reptilian bodies as the adults, but without the astonishingly muscular limbs of a full-grown LP.

Those black vertical pupils. Nightmare stuff.

Julie watches for only a few seconds. Sees there's no hope. Then she turns and continues running and doesn't stop for a very long time.

By the time Control is done with this memory, the worst of the carnage will probably be cut. They've learned their own lesson about that. Too many people still get off on snuff films. It's been interfering with the work.

Control might make other changes. By the time they're done, Julie Trident might not even appear in her own memory at all.

That's happened before, although Tim isn't sure why.

But he knows from Colonel Jenks that Julie's role is vital to all concerned. Whether it's now or some time in the future, Colonel Jenks never exactly said.

It doesn't matter anyway. Tim will help Julie in whatever way he can.

That's how he's wired now. And it gives him a purpose he never felt before in most of his thirty-three years.

Tim has watched enough of this memory. He scrubs any trace of his access to it and returns to his normal tasks.

Some time later, maybe tonight while Julie Trident is sleeping, Tim will follow protocol and slip the memory out of her mind and deposit it straight into Control's vast library.

But he's in no hurry to take it from her. He hates that he has to take it at all. He'll stall as long as he can before Randy Mitchell reminds him to cache all the current memories and wait for Julie Trident's next mission.

7

Julie wanders the halls of the Factory.

Now that her arm is normal again, she's hungry and could use some coffee.

She finds the cafeteria on Level Three. ("Try the cinnamon buns," Dr. Tognocci advises her. "They only make them there.")

Julie orders a slice of cheese pizza, a cinnamon bun as wide as her hand, and a cup of black coffee that smells slightly acidic to her nose, but Dr. Tognocci warned her that was the effect of the shot.

"The sugar will clear you out soon," she told her back in the infirmary. "Seems to reset the nerves."

Julie carries her tray to the end of a long empty table and digs in, savoring the bready texture of the pizza.

"Me again," Dr. Tognocci says. She has a cup of coffee of her own. She takes the seat next to Julie.

Julie pushes over the plate with the cinnamon bun and

hands Dr. Tognocci a knife. To her credit, the doctor doesn't protest. She slices off a section and takes her fair share.

"I'm sure you have your protocol," Dr. Tognocci says quietly.

Julie nods and takes another bite of pizza.

"But it takes an awfully long time for information to filter down," the doctor says. "I'd appreciate it if you could tell me more."

Julie wonders why they didn't have this conversation while she was still in the infirmary. But then she remembers the nurse was always there. Maybe this really is as much privacy as Dr. Tognocci can find.

"Such as?" Julie murmurs.

"How far away they were. How many of them. What they smelled like—specifically. Just anything you can think of right before they attacked."

It's a relief, actually. Not to be asked about what happened after. That's what she'll have to detail out in her report. All the butchery.

But to talk about the before instead. She's happy to linger there.

Julie eats some of the restorative cinnamon bun and tells Dr. Tognocci everything she wants to know. She can feel the memories flowing out of the left side of her brain, while the duplicate file over on the right stays quiet and hidden in its secret cave.

With each question the doctor asks, the details grow more vivid and intense. When they're done Julie might have to recopy the memory in its new enhanced version.

"Did the others seem ... frozen, in a way?" Dr. Tognocci asks her. "Paralyzed?"

Julie thinks back. About the slow reactions of the scientists and the soldiers, despite her efforts to rouse them.

"Maybe," Julie says. Now that she thinks about it, the confusion that she saw, especially with Dr. Ash, could have been caused by something external, some kind of neurobiological agent, rather than from Control's internal tampering with Dr. Ash's memories. Maybe they didn't remove the information Dr. Ash needed to stay safe. Maybe Julie has assumed the wrong thing.

"Was that what happened to my arm?" Julie asks the doctor. "Some kind of neurological attack?"

"Maybe," Dr. Tognocci answers. "That's why I needed to talk to you. I'm still trying to figure this all out."

Julie thinks about how it went down. How she immediately ran and kept on running. "So what would have happened to me if I'd stayed there any longer? Would I have been able to leave at all?"

"Hate to say it," Dr. Tognocci says, "but right now your guess is as good as mine."

8

Tim Cudahey checks Julie Trident's stats. She's still awake, her vitals are normal again, so the pain and numbness must be gone.

"Trident?" Randy Mitchell asks him during one of the supervisory sweeps.

"Stable," Tim answers.

"Good, good." Randy Mitchell peers over Tim's shoulder at the various numbers and dots on the computer screen.

"Utah?" he asks, noticing her location.

"Yes, sir." Tim thinks fast. He's the one who told Julie to go there. It wasn't supposed to be his call. "Trident must have heard of the serum they've been working on at the Factory. It's supposed to counteract some of the toxins released by the LPs."

"Then she was exposed?" Randy Mitchell asks. There's a note of warning in his voice.

"No, sir," Tim says. "It must just be for research purposes.

I'll find out soon enough. I assume she'll sleep within the next few hours."

"Yes, all right," Mitchell says. "Keep me apprised."

The supervisor leaves and the heavy door glides shut.

The Control engineer sitting next to Tim has obviously heard it all.

She bumps his left arm. He looks over at her, surprised. Her name is Carmen and she's a few years younger than he is, although she's been working here longer.

They rarely interact, the engineers. There's always too much going on with the screens in front of them to notice the humans sitting in living flesh all around them.

"Careful," she says quietly. She looks to her own left, makes sure no one is listening. "They'll quarantine her. Did it to one of my guys last week. I'm not sure he's ever going to get out."

Tim leans closer to her. This is not good news. It's the first he's heard of it, although Randy Mitchell and Carmen might have carried on such a conversation in the open right beside him and Tim was too busy at the time to pay attention.

"What should I do?" he whispers.

Carmen points at his screen. "Skew the data, idiot."

9

Julie stretches out on the soft queen-sized bed inside one of the small guest rooms kept by the Factory. She feels fine, she could have left by now, but she finds she's in no hurry to return to her base.

The room is clean and modern and sparsely-furnished with just a bed, a small nightstand, a narrow desk and accompanying chair, and a bathroom with a simple shower stall. She has stayed in one of the rooms here before on five other occasions, after successful missions in the nearby mountains.

She hates to feel like she's hiding out right now, licking her wounds, so instead she views it as a chance for further research.

Dr. Tognocci has promised to share some of the other reports that have come to her in private conversations.

Why Control doesn't disseminate all the available information immediately to all concerned, Julie can't understand.

It's her life and the lives of others out in the field that depend on the most current knowledge any of them have.

But then she thinks of what Tim Cudahey told her that first time he invaded her head.

Why it was important for Julie to keep her own inviolate copy of her memories, somewhere where she can return to them whenever she needs.

She is just a tool to be used. They all are. For the benefit of scientific knowledge. Julie is all right with that, in principle. It's a proper use of her abilities and training.

She remembers one of her professors at the University of Montana where she did her biology undergrad telling the class about the historical progress of science.

"It's not new knowledge that pushes us ahead," he said. "It's the fact that the old scientists who refuse to change their minds finally start dying off."

He said if you did a survey of all the great scientific breakthroughs throughout the centuries, you'd see that the real innovations might have been discovered by a few geniuses here and there, but generally there came a time when scientists in their particular fields just started to understand that what they thought up until then simply wasn't correct.

"But the scientific community," her professor told the class, "they like to keep control. Even Albert Einstein was like that. He hated giving in to quantum mechanics. He fought it for the longest time.

"You can understand why," he said. "If you're a scientist at the top of your field, you've probably spent your whole professional life chasing down some pet theory of yours.

And here comes some young upstart to laugh in your face and tell you you're wrong."

But then the old guard dies out, her professor said. And new knowledge just becomes accepted. Because the younger generation of scientists believed the new truth all along.

Julie lies on the comfortable bed and lets her gaze rest on the clean white ceiling above. That lecture from her professor had a profound effect on her at the time. She tries to keep the lesson in mind whenever she's feeling certain that she understands one of her own scientific conclusions.

What if she's wrong? That's the question she asks herself as frequently as she remembers to do it. It's a hard bit of mental exercise, because her professor is right, we all love our theories. We all love to believe we already know so much and can move on to the vast territory of more unknowns.

But what if she's wrong right now, and needs to start over with some of her assumptions?

The peach-colored youngsters never attack.

What if they do? What if they were just distracted today, and she was foolish to assume they wouldn't? She can't afford to let down her guard. If she sees an LP of any age or color, she needs to assume the alien will kill her.

Weapons can protect her.

What if they can't? What if the LPs emit some kind of mind-altering, body-paralyzing nerve toxin now, and so carrying a gun won't help at all? By the time they're near enough for you to smell them, it's too late. You're dead.

Her arm is healed. She won't have any more trouble with it.

But what if she does? What if her arm becomes paralyzed? Can she still do her work?

What if her exposure to the LPs' toxin shows up in her body some time later from now, when she's not expecting it?

Is there any cure? Will she be able to get to it in time?

Or will she find herself out in the wilderness one day, staring into the cold, sick eyes of the reptiles, and know that she's about to be torn apart limb from limb, and all she can do is stand frozen and let it happen?

She would never admit this to Tim Cudahey or anyone else, but a part of Julie wants to bed down like a deer right now, here in the safety of the thick cover of trees. To stay here for a while, help Dr. Tognocci advance her research, knowing that the doctor's solutions might benefit Julie directly.

But it's like the old saying: A ship is safe in harbor, but that's not what ships are built for.

Julie slips her good left arm behind her head and stares at the ceiling above her. She thinks about all of the elements of her life that have come together to bring her to exactly where she is right now.

What she's been built for. Why she possesses her particular set of skills.

PhD in biology. Specialty in predators. Extensive knowledge of the mountain ranges of the west, from Montana down to the Four Corners.

Firearms training.

Combat experience from a brief but memorable stint in the Marines.

A family history that maybe none of her colleagues has,

and that makes her feel uniquely connected to her work. Maybe some of it filtered down through her genes. Or maybe those claims of genetic inheritance in mankind are nothing but a myth.

But Julie still likes to believe it.

Her other grandfather, not the badass U.S. Marine, *Semper Fi*, but the one on her mother's side, he was a biologist, too. Then Julie's mother followed in his footsteps.

Ever since she was little, Julie wanted to live up to her family's example. Both the military and scientific sides.

To be a warrior-scientist. A scientist-soldier. Like the two different halves of her brain.

Joining them together across the linear divide. Making sure she always has access to both.

Julie groans herself back up to sitting. She's not tired and it's time to go. She wants to stay, but she can't. Ships aren't meant to remain in harbor.

She ties back her hair into a low ponytail and splashes water from the bathroom sink onto her face one more time.

She'll go back up two levels to the main hangar and see if she can catch a ride back to her own base.

But first she has one more stop to make.

She walks casually through the warren of corridors until she comes to a familiar door. She isn't supposed to be here, but it's a matter of protocol, not physical danger. A matter of security, too. No one is supposed to know who she is. Certain precautions have to be observed.

Julie assumes the door will be locked. But it will open for her. The first time she came to the Factory, years ago, she was able to add her own handprint to the lighted panel on the front of the door. She isn't able to come here often, but the door should still remember her and allow her inside.

Julie presses her hand against the blueish-white lighted panel and hears a click. The lock has released.

She opens the door to the laboratory. There is a woman sitting at the back of the room, peering closely at a computer screen.

The woman turns. Julie is surprised to see how thick her glasses are. Her eyesight must be getting worse. It pains Julie to see it.

But she smiles at the woman and hurries toward her across the room. Dr. Caroline Baird lets out a cry of delight —*Oh!*—and she stands up and opens her arms wide.

"Hi, Mom," Julie says, and she hugs her mother hard.

And just for now, just for a time, she lets herself rest.

She will return to the battle tomorrow.

Next in the Dove Season Universe
BELIEVER

- UFO biologist Dr. Travis Baird begins a new life away from prying eyes. But he can't outrun his past—or the alien intervention that changed him.
- Investigator Gina Firenzi knows she tapped into something strange the night she saved herself from getting shot. But what it was—and whether she can access again—is a mystery she needs to solve.
- Agency analyst Alice Kern wants the truth about her parents' murder—but only the truth. Is Gina's new source of information reliable? Or just another pretender claiming she can see into the past?
- Marnie Stemple has a new teacher. An alien woman with secrets Marnie longs to learn. But unlocking those secrets requires a leap into the unknown. Is Marnie brave enough to take it?
- Pilot Sharman Hix meets someone who challenges her view of the future—including the role Sharman intends to play in it.

The truth is already here. Get ready to believe it.

ABOUT THE AUTHOR

Robin Brande is an award-winning author, former trial attorney, black belt in martial arts, Reiki Master, and wilderness medic. Her outdoor adventures range from the Rocky Mountains to the Alps to Iceland.

She writes in multiple genres, including mystery, adventure, fantasy, science fiction, young adult, romance, and self-help.

For more information:
https://robinbrande.com/

For updates about upcoming installments of DOVE SEASON, along with previews and special discounts, subscribe to the Robin Brande newsletter: https://robinbrande.com/pages/subscribe.

MORE FROM ROBIN BRANDE

SHOW YOUR BOOK-LOVING STYLE!

AND SCIENCE LOVING, ART LOVING, DOG AND CAT LOVING, AND MORE...

Treat yourself to a soft, comfy, custom-made T-shirt designed by Robin Brande herself, inspired by her own books. You can see all of them at robinbrande.com/collections/t-shirts.

And here's a secret just for you: Use the discount code **READER10** at checkout to get **10% off any items in the store**. That means books, T-shirts, hoodies, mugs—whatever you'd like. Go ahead and treat yourself, book lover.

CERTIFIED
BOOK NERD
CERTIFIED
DOG NERD
CERTIFIED
SCIENCE NERD

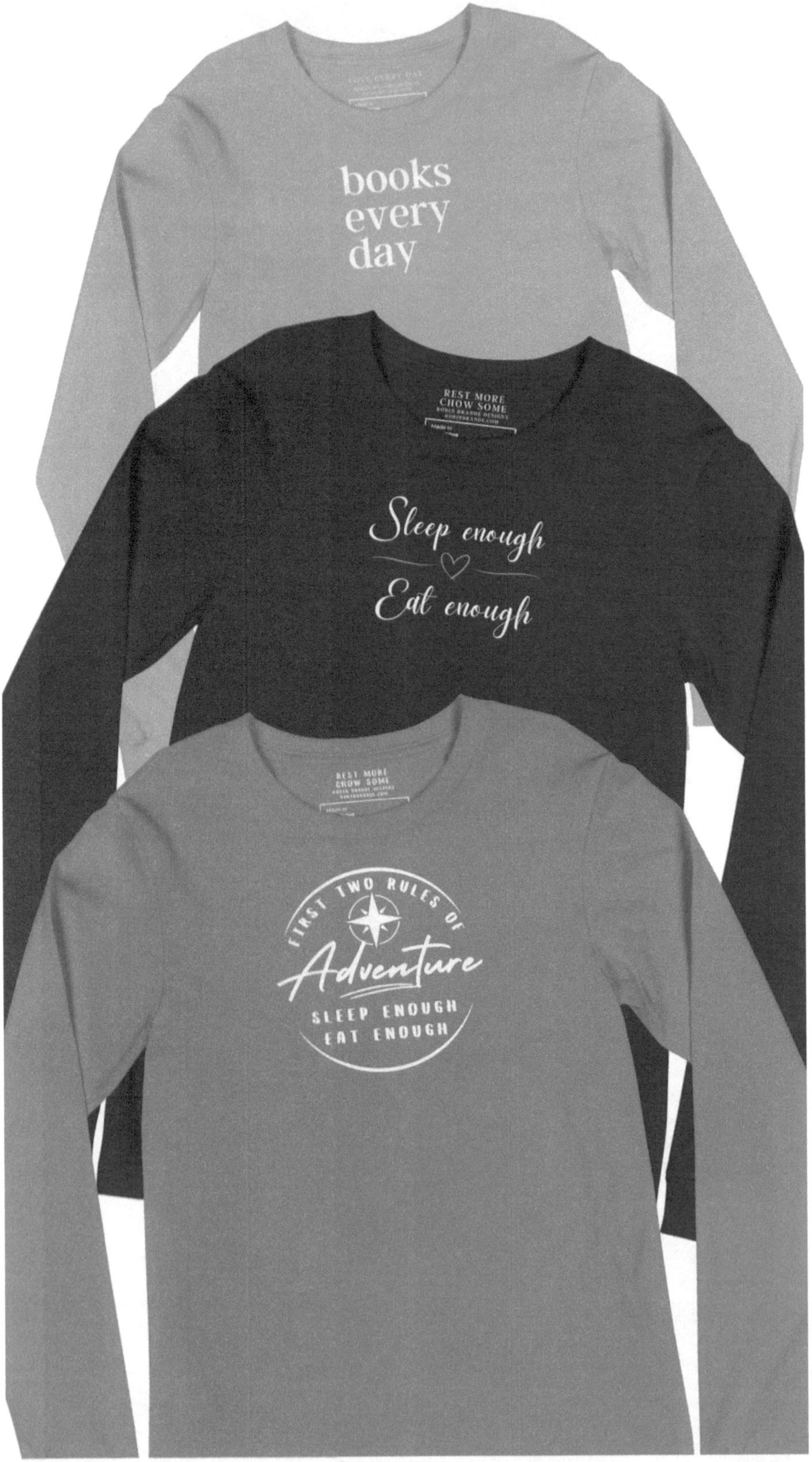
books
every
day
REST MORE
CHOW SOME
Sleep enough
Eat enough
REST MORE
CHOW SOME
FIRST TWO RULES OF
Adventure
SLEEP ENOUGH
EAT ENOUGH

Retired psychology professor Dr. Winifred Parsons spent decades studying the human psyche as a scientist and academic. But she also explored it from another angle: Winnie Parsons is clairvoyant.

Now Winnie uses her psi talent to help clients resolve mysteries that are outside the reach of standard investigations.

The path to justice might be twisted, but Winnie always finds a way.

Life after death, miracle healings, communication with other species...

- *The Water Healers*: A nurse investigates rumors of miracle healers in Mexico.
- *A Drop of Sweat*: A clairvoyant secretly uses her skills to unravel the mystery of who destroyed a scientist's lab.
- *The Refugees*: A volunteer helps the refugees fleeing a planetary disaster.
- *The Bridge*: A grieving widow refuses to believe her husband is gone forever.
- *The Outpost Away from the World*: A scientist returns to the off-the-grid cabin of her childhood and discovers the mysterious secret to her survival.

The mountains can dish it out. But that doesn't mean you have to take it.

- *On Red Mountain*: A woman must survive alone in the mountains after her husband is struck by lightning.
- *The Rescue*: A mountain hermit and his dog race to avert a coming disaster—one that the dog senses before anyone else.
- *Home Deer*: A mountain widow takes matters into her own hands to protect the nearby woodland creatures.
- *The Gold Hunter*: An injured climber's only hope for survival is a stranger who won't give up.
- *Taken at Rustler Pass*: A teen girl fights to survive against the stranger who wants her dead.

High school senior and amateur physicist Audie Masters discovers a parallel universe—along with a parallel version of herself.

It's the adventure of a lifetime.

Now all she has to do is survive it.

Read all four books in the exciting, mind-bending PARALLELOGRAM QUARTET. You'll never look at the universe or your own life the same way again.